Gospel of the Hebrews

by

Rick Wiatt

ISBN: 979-8-9932608-0-8 (Paperback)
Library of Congress Control Number: 2025920393
Any references to historical events, real people, or real places are used fictitiously. Names, characters, and places are products of the author's imagination.

Dedication

To the keepers of forgotten lore, the seekers of hidden truths, and the quiet guardians of history whose dedication illuminates the shadows of the past. May your persistence in the face of obscurity inspire all who dare to question, to explore, and to uncover the layers of time that shape our present understanding. This story is a testament to the relentless pursuit of knowledge, a journey undertaken not just through ancient texts and sacred sites, but through the very fabric of human belief and the enduring power of conviction. For every dusty manuscript waiting to be deciphered, for every forgotten whisper of a pivotal moment, and for the courage it takes to bring light to the darkness, this endeavor is humbly offered. May it serve as a reminder that the greatest discoveries often lie just beyond the edge of the known, waiting for those with the vision to see and the will to seek. To those who believe that the past holds not only lessons but also revelations that can redefine our future, this book is for you. It is a tribute to the insatiable curiosity that drives us to understand where we came from, and why it matters so profoundly. May your own journeys be filled with the wonder of revelation and the quiet satisfaction of unearthed wisdom.

Contents

Dedication 3

1: Echoes of the Past 5

2: The First Trail 23

3: The Serpent's Coil 31

4: The Alexandria Connection...45

5: The Sands of Time...56

6: The Ethiopian Enigma..64

7: The Herodian Connection 132

8: The Monastery of Silence 141

9: The Map of Stars 150

10: The Language of Symbols..161

11: The Guardian's Betrayal 170

12: The Path of Trials...177

13: The Revelation of the Hebrew....................................185

14: The Reckoning..192

15: The Dawn of Truth 200

Key Terms...209

References 211

1: Echoes of the Past

The air in Professor Elias Finch's study hung thick and still, a palpable testament to decades of accumulated wisdom and the scent of aging paper. Dust motes, golden and languid, pirouetted in the solitary shaft of sunlight that sliced through the leaded panes of the lancet window. The light filtered through panes of crimson and sapphire, painted fleeting, vibrant hues across the crammed shelves that climbed to the vaulted ceiling. Each leather-bound spine seemed to whisper tales of forgotten ages, of knowledge painstakingly preserved and occasionally lost to the ravages of time and indifference. It was here, amidst this comforting, scholarly chaos, that Evelyn Reed found herself once more, a familiar sanctuary that both soothed and stirred her soul.

Elias, his usually energetic frame settled into the worn depths of his favorite armchair, cradled a steaming mug of tea, his gaze fixed on a collection of brittle, yellowed fragments spread across the vast mahogany desk. The silence between them was not one of awkwardness but of shared anticipation, a stillness born of countless similar meetings, each preceding a plunge into the unknown. Their past endeavors, fraught with peril and intellectual puzzles, had forged an unbreakable bond, a partnership built on mutual respect and an insatiable hunger for uncovering the obscured truths of history.

"Remarkable, isn't it?" Elias's voice, though quiet, resonated with excitement. He gestured toward the fragments with a hand gnarled by age and by countless hours spent poring over ancient texts. "The precision of the script, the unusual composition of the ink... it all aligns with what we hypothesized after the incident in Jerusalem."

Evelyn leaned closer, her keen eyes scanning the delicate lines of script. The symbols, a curious blend of early Hebrew and something more elusive, felt like old friends, albeit ones that guarded their deeper secrets. "The isotopic analysis was conclusive, wasn't it? The carbon dating placed it firmly in the first century, possibly even earlier. But the metallurgy of the binding... it's unlike anything documented for that period." She ran a gloved fingertip over a small, almost imperceptible anomaly on one of the fragments, a faint raised symbol that seemed to hum with a hidden significance. "And this..."

"Precisely," Elias interjected, his eyes twinkling with the thrill of the chase. "It speaks of a craft, a knowledge, that simply vanished. Or, more accurately, was deliberately hidden. Each piece we recovered, each fragment that whispered its tale, only deepened the mystery surrounding the Gospel of the Hebrews."

He carefully adjusted a fragment that had shifted. "Remember the whispers we heard in that dusty Syriac monastery? The hushed pronouncements from the elder monks about texts considered too potent, too disruptive, for the nascent Church? They spoke of a narrative that offered a different perspective, a lineage of teachings that ran parallel, perhaps even counter, to the accepted doctrines."

Evelyn nodded, her mind replaying those hushed conversations, the grave warnings from men who had dedicated their lives to the preservation of sacred lore. The elders had been reluctant, their eyes filled with a mixture of reverence and fear. They spoke of a Hebrew root, a primordial understanding that the established narratives had sought to supplant, or worse, corrupt. The Gospel of the Hebrews, as Elias had christened it, was more than a historical curiosity; it was a potential seismic shift in the very foundations of religious history.

"The Council of Nicaea was a pivotal moment, wasn't it?" Evelyn mused, her gaze drifting to a bust of Constantine perched on a nearby bookshelf. "A period of consolidation, of standardization. But what was lost in that process? What truths were deemed inconvenient and subsequently buried?"

Elias sighed, a sound that carried the weight of centuries of scholarly debate. "That, my dear Evelyn, is the question that has driven countless scholars to madness, and perhaps a few to an untimely end. The canonization of scripture was a complex, often politically charged affair. Texts that did not align with the emerging orthodoxy, texts that offered a more egalitarian or mystical interpretation of the divine, were systematically suppressed. The Gospel of the Hebrews appears to be one such casualty, a testament to a more radical, earthbound form of spirituality."

He picked up another fragment, this one bearing a remarkably preserved illustration. It depicted a stylized tree, its branches reaching toward a celestial body, its roots plunging deep into stylized water. Within the leaves, faint, almost imperceptible symbols were etched, each one a miniature puzzle in itself.

"This symbology," Elias continued, his voice hushed with awe, "is reminiscent of early Gnostic texts, but with distinct Hebrew and possibly even Mesopotamian influences. The dualistic nature, the emphasis on gnosis, on direct, intuitive understanding of the divine... it suggests a lineage that predates the formal separation of what we now understand as Christianity and Judaism. It points toward a period of fertile, almost alchemical blending of spiritual ideas."

Evelyn carefully examined the illustration, her mind already whirring, making connections between ancient astrological charts, esoteric philosophies, and the cryptic verses they had painstakingly translated from the Jerusalem fragments. "The alignment here... it's not merely symbolic, is it? It mirrors certain celestial configurations. The position of Venus, the rising of Orion... it suggests a specific time, perhaps even a specific place, tied to astronomical observation."

"Indeed," Elias agreed, his enthusiasm undimmed by the sheer complexity of the task. "The fragment we found tucked within the bindings of that ancient psalter contained annotations that seemed to reference these very celestial bodies. It's as if the gospel itself is a celestial map, a guide not just to spiritual enlightenment, but to its own physical preservation."

He leaned back, a thoughtful frown creasing his brow. "The incident in Jerusalem... it was a stark reminder that we are not the only ones seeking these answers. The whispers we overheard, the hurried glances, the distinct impression that we were being observed... it cannot be dismissed. There are forces, Evelyn, deeply entrenched forces, that have a vested interest in keeping the Gospel of the Hebrews buried."

Evelyn shivered, despite the warmth of the study. The memory of the shadowed alley, the glint of something metallic in the gloom, the unsettling feeling of being watched by unseen eyes, was still vivid. They had escaped, but only by the narrowest of margins, and the lingering sense of unease never truly left.

"The individuals who intervened... they were not common thieves," she stated firmly. "Their movements were too precise, their methods too efficient. They knew exactly what they were looking for, and more importantly, what they were preventing us from finding."

"They were protectors," Elias corrected, his tone somber. "Protectors of a secret that has evidently been guarded for millennia. And now, it seems, our renewed pursuit has drawn their attention once more. This gathering, this review of the fragments, is not merely a scholarly exercise. It is the commencement of a new expedition, and I fear, a far more perilous one than any we have undertaken before."

He gestured to the desk, where the fragments lay scattered like fallen leaves. "The clues are fragmented, scattered across continents and centuries. But they converge, don't they? They point toward a path, a grand narrative arc that winds through the very heart of human spiritual and intellectual history. From the dusty shelves of our own esteemed universities to the sunbaked landscapes of the Levant, then perhaps to the intellectual crucible of Alexandria, and beyond..."

"To the very origins of belief itself," Evelyn finished softly. The scent of old parchment mingled with the subtle aroma of Elias's pipe tobacco, a comforting yet potent reminder of the task ahead. The weight of their previous discoveries, the burden of knowledge, settled upon her shoulders, but it was a familiar burden, one she embraced. The fragments on the desk were more than just pieces of paper; they were invitations, beckoning them toward a truth that had been deliberately obscured, a truth that had the power to rewrite the very paradigms of their understanding. The quiet study, usually a haven of predictable scholarship, now felt like the precipice of a new, exhilarating, and dangerous adventure.

The chime of the grandfather clock in the hallway, a sonorous cadence that had marked the passing of countless hours in Elias's study, faded into silence, leaving the room once again to the hushed rustle of paper and the quiet breathing of its occupants. Evelyn traced the outline of a symbol on a fragment, a stylized serpent coiled around a star, its scales rendered with microscopic intricacy. "The incident in Jerusalem was a clear signal, Elias. We're not alone in this pursuit. Whoever those individuals were, they weren't merely trying to stop us from recovering the fragments; they were actively trying to seize them. That particular piece, the one with the astronomical annotations, seemed to be their primary target."

Elias nodded, his brow furrowed. "Indeed. Their methods were disturbingly efficient, and their knowledge of our operations, or at least our presence, was uncanny. It suggests a network, Evelyn, a deeply embedded organization with an interest in keeping the Gospel of the Hebrews hidden, and with the resources to enforce that secrecy. The question remains: who are they, and what is it about this particular text that makes it so vital to conceal?" He picked up a small, leaden disc, no larger than a coin, its surface covered in an array of interlocking symbols that seemed to shift and rearrange themselves under the light. "This, of course, was recovered separately. A gift, shall we say, from an anonymous benefactor who sought us out in Prague."

Evelyn's eyes widened slightly. She recalled the hushed meeting in a dimly lit Bohemian café, the air thick with the scent of roasted coffee beans and pipe smoke, a stark contrast to the scholarly tranquility of Elias's study. The man who had approached them, a shadowy figure whose face remained largely obscured by the brim of his hat and the perpetual twilight of the establishment, had been a creature of profound mystery. He had spoken in a low, gravelly voice, each word carefully chosen, laced with an urgency that belied his outwardly calm demeanor.

"He was a man of few words, Elias," Evelyn recalled, the memory still vivid. "He spoke of an ancient order, sworn to protect certain truths. Truths that, in his words, could unravel the fabric of established belief. He claimed to be a messenger, an emissary from those who understood the true significance of what we were pursuing. He pressed this into my hand with a warning: 'The past is not merely a story; it is a weapon. And this gospel is a sword.'"

She picked up the leaden disc, its surface cool and strangely smooth against her gloved fingers. The symbols etched upon it were unlike any she had encountered in her extensive studies of ancient scripts. They possessed a fluidity, a curvilinear quality that hinted at a language far older than the cuneiform of Mesopotamia or the hieroglyphs of Egypt. There were elements that vaguely resembled early Proto Sinaitic script, yet they were imbued with a geometric precision, a mathematical elegance that suggested a sophisticated understanding of cosmic order.

"The man mentioned a lineage," Evelyn continued, turning the disc over in her hand. "A chain of custodians who had passed down knowledge, and the artifacts associated with it, for generations. He said they had watched us, that they recognized our dedication and our discretion. But he also warned of, others. Others who sought to exploit this knowledge, to twist its meaning for their own ends. He called them the Shadow Scribes."

Elias leaned forward, his gaze fixed on the disc. "The Shadow Scribes. A rather evocative moniker. And what was the nature of this artifact? What did your messenger claim it represented?"

"He called it a Key of Knowing," Evelyn replied, her voice tinged with awe. "He said it was one of several, each designed to unlock a deeper understanding of the Gospel of the Hebrews. He explained that the symbols were not merely decorative, but a form of cipher, tied to specific celestial alignments. This particular disc, he claimed, corresponded to a conjunction of planets that occurred in the first century, a rare alignment that marked a significant moment in the gospel's history."

She held the disc closer to the light filtering through the window. One of the symbols, a spiral radiating outward from a central point, seemed to pulse with an inner luminescence. It was subtle, almost imperceptible, but undeniably present. "He implied that this alignment was not just astrological, but somehow imprinted itself upon the text, leaving a trace, a signature."

"Fascinating," Elias breathed, his scholarly curiosity igniting. "A celestial cipher. It aligns with our observations of the astronomical notations on the Jerusalem fragments. It suggests a deliberate encoding, a method of safeguarding the gospel's most profound secrets, not through physical concealment alone, but through a layered system of interpretive keys." He gestured to a shelf laden with ancient astronomical charts and codices. "The ancients often viewed the heavens as a grand library, a cosmic repository of divine knowledge. To encode a text within the very language of the stars is an audacious, yet profoundly elegant approach."

"The emissary also spoke of a location," Evelyn added, her gaze sweeping across the cluttered desk, as if searching for a misplaced piece of the puzzle. "A place where the Gospel of the Hebrews was first transcribed, a sanctuary of sorts, before it was dispersed. He was vague, but he used the term House of Whispers. He said that further keys, further fragments, could be found there, but that it was heavily guarded by the Shadow Scribes."

Elias mused on the phrase, "The House of Whispers," the words carrying a mythical weight. "It sounds like a place steeped in esoteric lore. Could it be a monastic cell, a hidden scriptorium, perhaps even a forgotten temple?"

"He was adamant about the danger, Elias," Evelyn stressed, her voice hardening with resolve. "He made it clear that the Shadow Scribes were not merely guardians of a secret; they were active participants in its suppression. They would stop at nothing to prevent its rediscovery. He hinted that they had already silenced others who had come too close, men and women of learning, who had dared to follow the whispers of this forbidden text."

The memory of the near fatal encounter in Jerusalem flashed through her mind, the sudden ambush, the swift and brutal efficiency of their attackers. They had been too prepared, too skilled, too intent on their objective. It was not the random violence of street thugs, but the calculated precision of seasoned operatives. They had been fortunate to escape, but the encounter had left an indelible mark, a chilling realization of the forces at play.

"The emissary also alluded to the nature of the Gospel of the Hebrews itself," Evelyn continued, her voice dropping lower. "He suggested that it was not merely a religious text, but a compendium of lost knowledge, encompassing philosophy, astronomy, and even a form of early science that predated much of what we consider modern discovery. He spoke of a primordial understanding of the universe, a perspective that was deliberately suppressed by later religious authorities because it challenged their established hierarchies and doctrines."

Elias's eyes gleamed with the familiar fire of intellectual pursuit, a spark that even the most daunting of challenges could not extinguish. "A challenge to established doctrines... that would certainly explain the fervor of its suppression. History is replete with examples of knowledge deemed too dangerous, too subversive, for the prevailing order. Texts that offered alternative narratives, that questioned authority, were often relegated to the realm of heresy and systematically eradicated."

He leaned back, steepling his fingers. "Consider the Library of Alexandria, Evelyn. A beacon of ancient learning, its destruction a catastrophic loss. But even within surviving collections, there were undoubtedly texts deemed too radical, too unsettling, to be widely disseminated. The Gospel of the Hebrews, if it indeed contains such profound and potentially disruptive insights, would have been a prime target for any entity seeking to maintain a particular ideological or religious status quo."

"The emissary's urgency was palpable," Evelyn said, her gaze returning to the leaden disc. "He presented this as a critical juncture. He believes that the time is approaching when the Gospel of the Hebrews will be revealed, and that its rediscovery will have profound implications for the world. He fears that if it falls into the wrong hands, into the hands of those who would twist its message for their own purposes, the consequences could be catastrophic."

"The Shadow Scribes," Elias echoed, the name now carrying a greater weight of menace. "And our enigmatic benefactor from Prague, who appears to be aligned with this ancient order. It's a complex tapestry, Evelyn, woven with threads of history, theology, and perhaps something far more ancient and powerful." He tapped a finger on the desk near the collection of fragments. "These pieces, scattered as they are, are more than just historical curiosities. They are beacons, guiding us through a labyrinth of secrecy and deception. And with the addition of this Key of Knowing, our path, though fraught with peril, becomes a little clearer."

Evelyn nodded, a sense of anticipation mixed with trepidation settling over her. The study, once a sanctuary of quiet contemplation, now felt like the launching point of an epic quest, a journey into the very heart of forgotten history. The whispers of the past, once faint echoes, were growing louder, more insistent, beckoning them toward a truth that had been deliberately buried, a truth that promised to reshape their understanding of the world. The air crackled with the unspoken promise of discovery, and the chilling certainty that the Shadow Scribes would not be far behind. The game had indeed begun, and the stakes were higher than ever before. The very foundations of historical and religious understanding hung in the balance, waiting to be irrevocably altered by the unveiling of the Gospel of the Hebrews.

Outside, the faintest of breezes, carrying the scent of ozone and something metallic, snaked through the narrow alleyway. It was a scent that had become unnervingly familiar to Elias, a preamble to the disquiet that always preceded his nocturnal excursions. He pulled the collar of his worn trench coat tighter, the rough wool a meager defense against the chill that had nothing to do with the late autumn air. Below, the muted glow of the city spread like spilled ink, a thousand tiny fires that seemed to beckon and warn in equal measure. His gaze, sharp and accustomed to piercing the murk, swept across the illuminated windows of the Lyceum's upper floors, where Evelyn and Elias would still be poring over their newfound treasures. They were so close, he knew. So agonizingly close to unlocking the secrets that had been meticulously guarded for millennia.

He adjusted the worn leather strap of the satchel slung across his chest. Inside, nestled among faded maps and cryptic notes, lay his own contribution to this unfolding mystery: a collection of painstakingly crafted forgeries designed to sow seeds of doubt and misdirection. It was delicate work, a dance on the precipice of discovery, and one he had perfected over years of clandestine operations. His current assignment was simple, yet fraught with peril: to monitor the progress of the two academics, to ensure their path did not stray too close to certain guarded truths, and, if necessary, to intervene without leaving a trace.

His vantage point offered a discreet panorama of the Lyceum's exterior. The grand old building, usually a beacon of quiet scholarship, now felt like a stage set for a drama of unseen forces. He had been observing them for three days, ever since the anonymous courier, cloaked in the anonymity of the city's teeming crowds, had delivered the leaden disc to Evelyn. He had seen the spark of curiosity ignite, then blossom into the consuming fire of intellectual pursuit. He had watched, with a mixture of admiration and apprehension, as Elias's encyclopedic mind grappled with the celestial ciphers and Evelyn's linguistic prowess unraveled the ancient scripts. They were brilliant, undeniably so. Their synergy was a force to be reckoned with, a potent combination that threatened to unearth truths a select few had dedicated their lives to burying.

Elias, moved with the practiced silence of a phantom, his footsteps barely disturbing the fallen leaves scattered across the cobbled lane. He paused at the mouth of a narrow passage, a sliver of darkness between two imposing brick buildings. The air here was heavy and stagnant, carrying the faint acrid tang of something long since burned. It was here, tucked away from the main thoroughfare, that his own network operated. He reached into his coat pocket, his fingers brushing against a smooth, cool surface. A small obsidian charm, intricately carved with a symbol that was both familiar and unsettling, a coiled serpent biting its own tail, but with wings. This was the mark of the Silent Order, the custodians of the sacred texts, the guardians against what they perceived as profane intrusion.

He stopped, his senses suddenly sharpening. A glint of light, too deliberate to be accidental, caught his eye from a darkened window on the third floor of the Lyceum. It was a reflection, momentarily blinding, as if a shard of mirror had been held at the precise angle of a distant light source. It was a signal, a silent confirmation that their own watchers were also in place. The game, as always, was being played on multiple levels, with unseen players moving across the board with meticulous precision. He lowered his gaze, feigning casual observation of the city lights, while his mind processed the implications. Evelyn and Elias were not merely uncovering history; they were disturbing a delicate equilibrium that had been maintained for centuries.

He continued his circuit, his route taking him past a dimly lit café, its patrons a blend of late-night workers and solitary figures nursing lukewarm drinks. The low murmur of conversation drifted out, a tapestry of everyday concerns. Elias filtered through the sounds, his ear attuned to anything that deviated from the norm. Then he heard it, a brief, hushed exchange in a language as ancient as it was guttural, a dialect rarely spoken outside of clandestine gatherings. It was a tongue laced with the dry rustle of parchment and the clatter of iron, a language that spoke of oaths sworn in shadowed chambers and allegiance pledged to forgotten doctrines. He could not discern the exact words, but the cadence, the clipped, urgent tones, spoke of reconnaissance and reporting. Two men, seated at a corner table, their faces obscured by the gloom, were evidently connected to the same currents that Elias himself navigated. They were not rivals in the traditional sense, but fellow travelers on a path defined by secrecy and the deliberate manipulation of knowledge.

He reached into his coat again, this time producing a folded newspaper, its pages crisp and unread. As he passed the café, he casually dropped it onto the empty chair beside the two men. It landed with a soft thud, a silent acknowledgment, a gesture of recognition within the hidden fraternity. They did not look up, did not acknowledge his presence, but Elias knew the paper would be collected, its contents scrutinized for any subtle messages or confirmations.

The pursuit of the Gospel of the Hebrews was not a solitary endeavor. It was a vast, intricate web, spun by hands that rarely saw the light of day. The leaden disc, the celestial conjunction, the House of Whispers, these were but threads in a much larger tapestry, a tapestry woven from centuries of power, faith, and carefully curated ignorance. Evelyn and Elias, in their earnest quest for truth, had stumbled into the heart of this ancient conspiracy. They believed they were on the cusp of a monumental discovery, a revelation that would rewrite the accepted historical narrative. And in a way, they were. But they were also on a collision course with an organization whose very existence was predicated on ensuring that such revelations remained buried.

Elias continued his vigil, moving through the labyrinthine streets of the city. He saw other subtle signs, a shadow detaching itself from a deeper shadow, a brief flicker of movement in a window that was otherwise dark, a discarded matchbook lying incongruously on a deserted bench, its surface bearing the stylized imprint of a falcon in flight, its eyes two tiny, unblinking emeralds. The falcon. That was the insignia of the Ophidian Guard, an auxiliary force sworn to the Silent Order, their purpose to intercept and neutralize any threats to the established order. They were the enforcers, the ones who dealt with more permanent solutions.

He reached the riverfront, the dark water flowing sluggishly beneath the bridges. The air here was colder, carrying the briny tang of the sea. He found a secluded spot beneath an old, skeletal oak tree, its branches gnarled and reaching like bony fingers toward the starless sky. Here, he opened a small, encrypted device, its screen glowing with an ethereal blue light. He began to transmit his report, his fingers flying across the miniature keyboard. Subject Alpha and Subject Beta making significant progress. Celestial alignment identified. Potential geographical coordinates emerging. Observation ongoing. Counterintelligence elements active in the vicinity. He paused, considering his next move. The agents he had seen, the subtle signs of surveillance, they were all connected. Evelyn and Elias had not only attracted the attention of those who wished to keep the gospel hidden, but they had also drawn the focus of others, those who, like Elias, operated in the shadows, their own motives often as opaque as the texts they sought.

He closed the device, the blue light vanishing as if it had never been. He looked back toward the Lyceum, a dark silhouette against the bruised twilight sky. The warmth of their study, the shared excitement of discovery, the thrill of piecing together fragments of lost history seemed distant now, an innocence neither of them could afford. The House of Whispers was not just a destination; it was a focal point, a vortex that drew in all who sought its secrets. And as the city slept, the unseen forces that revolved around Evelyn and Elias's pursuit began to stir, their ancient machines shifting into motion. The shadows were not just gathering; they were preparing to act.

The hushed reverence of the Lyceum's library had always been a sanctuary for Elias Finch. Here, amidst the scent of aged paper and binding glue, he found solace from the clamor of the outside world, and more importantly, from the echoing silence within his own soul. Yet lately, the very air of this hallowed space seemed to hum with a disquiet that mirrored his inner turmoil. The leaden disc, now locked away in a climate-controlled vault, felt less like a key to unlocking history and more like a Pandora's Box, its contents threatening to spill out and contaminate the ordered world he had so painstakingly built. His days were consumed by deciphering celestial charts, by tracing the forgotten constellations etched onto the disc's surface, but his nights were a battlefield. Sleep offered little respite, plagued by fragmented visions, starlit deserts, cryptic pronouncements whispered in tongues he could not quite place, and the overwhelming sensation of being watched.

Evelyn Reed, in contrast, approached the enigma with a ferocity that bordered on recklessness. Her academic reputation, built painstakingly over years of meticulous research, felt suddenly fragile, like a delicate glassblower's creation poised on the edge of a precipice. The discovery of the disc had reignited a fire banked low for years, ever since the politically charged atmosphere at the university had stifled her groundbreaking work on ancient Aramaic dialects. She recalled the hushed whispers, the accusations of unorthodox interpretations, the subtle but persistent pressure to conform. Her mentor, Professor Armitage, a man whose own career had been tarnished by challenging prevailing narratives, had warned her then to tread carefully. "The past," he'd told her, "is not always a comforting place. Some doors are best left unopened." Those words echoed now with chilling prescience.

The Gospel of the Hebrews, as the preliminary analyses suggested it might be, promised to overturn centuries of accepted doctrine, to rewrite the very foundations of Western civilization. But the path to such a revelation was fraught with peril. She had received an anonymous letter, slipped beneath her office door, a single stark sentence scrawled in an elegant, archaic script: Some truths are best left to the dust. The handwriting mirrored the hand of the same scribe who had penned her father's final, cryptic letter, discovered among his belongings after his untimely death years ago. His death had been ruled an accident, but Evelyn had always suspected otherwise. Her father, a brilliant but controversial linguist, had been on the cusp of a monumental discovery. The disc, the letters, her father's fate, these were threads of a single, terrifying tapestry, and she was now inextricably caught within its weave.

Their collaboration, once fueled by shared intellectual curiosity, now carried an unspoken undercurrent of dread. Elias found himself watching Evelyn with a newfound intensity, not just as a colleague but as a fellow traveler on a perilous path. He saw the shadows beneath her eyes, the way her jaw tightened when she spoke of her father, the flicker of defiance that burned brightest when confronted by danger. He recognized in her a shared burden, a sense of inherited responsibility that went beyond academic pursuit. He remembered their first meeting, years ago, at a dusty symposium on ancient cartography. Evelyn, then a bright-eyed graduate student, had boldly challenged a renowned historian's interpretation of a Ptolemaic map. Elias, already a rising star in his field, had been captivated by her audacity and her unshakable conviction. They had bonded over a shared disdain for complacency, a mutual respect for the pursuit of knowledge no matter how uncomfortable the truths it unearthed.

But complacency was the least of their worries now.

One evening, as they worked late in the Lyceum's observation room, the vast holographic star chart flickering before them, Elias confessed his anxieties. "Evelyn," he began, his voice barely above a whisper, the hum of the projector the only other sound in the cavernous space. "I've been troubled. This disc, the texts, they speak of a power, a presence, that feels profoundly unsettling. It's as if we're peering into something ancient, something that was deliberately hidden for a reason." He gestured toward the projected cosmos. "My faith, Evelyn, in the sanctity of knowledge, in the idea that all truths are meant to be revealed... it's wavering."

Evelyn turned from the display, her expression unreadable in the dim light. She understood the unspoken. Elias, a man of meticulous scientific inquiry, had always possessed a quiet, almost apologetic faith, a deep-seated belief in the inherent order of the universe. To see her that shaken was to witness a profound personal crisis. She saw it as a reflection of her own unease, a confirmation that their journey was leading them into territory far more treacherous than any historical text could describe. "I understand, Elias," she said softly. "I've had similar doubts. My father used to talk about the dangers of cursed knowledge. He believed some discoveries came with a price, a price that could be paid by more than just the discoverer." She hesitated, her gaze drifting toward the window, the distant city lights a blur. "He died searching for something similar. Something tied to the very origins of faith and heresy. And I think this disc might be the key to understanding what happened to him."

The revelation hung between them. Elias's eyes widened, comprehension replacing apprehension. He had known Evelyn's father was a linguist, had heard whispers of his controversial theories, but he had not grasped the personal weight behind Evelyn's pursuit. This was not merely an academic endeavor for her. It was a quest for answers, a desperate attempt to vindicate her father and understand his fate. His own philosophical quandaries now seemed small compared to Evelyn's raw need for truth and closure.

He reached out, his hand hovering before resting gently on her arm. "Evelyn, I had no idea. If this is tied to your father's work, to his death, then we must proceed with the utmost care. This is no longer just about uncovering a historical artifact. It's about justice, perhaps?"

A faint, sad smile touched Evelyn's lips. "Perhaps. Or perhaps it's about preventing others from suffering the same fate. My father was accused of heresy, Elias. His research threatened to dismantle the pillars of established doctrine. They silenced him, and I believe this disc is what he was looking for, the proof he needed." Her gaze hardened. "If this gospel is real, if it reveals what I suspect it might, then it's not just history that's at stake. It's the control of narrative, the power to define truth itself. And that's a power many are willing to kill for."

Elias absorbed her words, the pieces clicking into place with chilling finality. He saw now the immense personal weight Evelyn carried, the legacy of her father's silenced voice. His own intellectual curiosity had always been tempered by a belief in objectivity, a detachment that allowed him to analyze without becoming too entangled. But Evelyn's involvement, her deeply personal connection to the mystery, had irrevocably altered the landscape. He found himself unexpectedly protective, his academic admiration evolving into something more profound, a shared sense of purpose forged in the crucible of shared danger.

He recalled an old phrase from his theological studies: Lux in tenebris lucet, et tenebrae eam non comprehenderunt. Light shines in the darkness, and the darkness comprehends it not. He had always interpreted it in a spiritual sense. Now, he wondered if it referred to a different kind of light, a historical truth so blinding, so revolutionary, that those who guarded the shadows would stop at nothing to extinguish it.

He looked at Evelyn, at the fierce determination in her eyes, and knew his own journey had irrevocably shifted. His crisis of faith was no longer an abstract debate but a tangible struggle against forces that had already taken lives. Their personal journeys, their doubts, their burdens, were no longer side stories. They were becoming the very spine of the narrative unfolding around them. The Gospel of the Hebrews was not merely a text; it was a catalyst, a mirror reflecting the deepest fears and most profound desires of those who dared to seek its truth.

And beyond the walls of the Lyceum, the shadows were moving.

2: The First Trail

The crackle of the parchment under Elias's gloved fingers was a familiar comfort, a sound that usually soothed his academic soul. Yet this time the ancient script whispered of more than facts; it hinted at secrets, at truths deliberately hidden. He traced the faded ink, following the intricate patterns of a star chart that mirrored the celestial configurations described in Evelyn's fragmented visions.

The Lyceum, once a sanctuary, now felt like a gilded cage, trapping him with the weight of the leaden disc and the fears that clung to it like dust. Sleep offered no true rest. His nights were a torment of fractured dreams. He saw star-strewn deserts stretching to distant horizons, heard cryptic pronouncements in archaic tongues that resonated in his bones, and felt the chilling certainty of being observed by something unseen.

His faith in the steady progress of knowledge, a foundation he had always trusted, was eroding. A question, small but corrosive, lodged itself in his mind: Was he unearthing something humanity was never meant to comprehend? The doubt gnawed at him, a pressure in his chest that turned each breath deliberate and heavy.

Evelyn, by contrast, met the enigma with fire that bordered on recklessness. The edifice of her academic reputation, built over years of relentless research, now felt fragile, like blown glass on the verge of shattering. The discovery of the disc had rekindled a dormant passion, smothered long ago under university politics and whispered accusations of "unorthodox interpretation."

She remembered her mentor, Professor Armitage, warning her in that dim office years ago. "The past," he had said with a voice worn by regret, "is not always a comforting place. Some doors are best left unopened." Those words returned to her now with an unnerving precision. The artifact, believed to be tied to the Gospel of the Hebrews, promised to overturn centuries of doctrine. The path to revelation, however, was perilous.

One letter sealed her resolve: a single line on elegant parchment slipped beneath her door. Some truths are best left to the dust. The handwriting mirrored that of her father's final cryptic note before his so-called "accidental" death. He had been on the verge of a discovery that was too monumental to ignore. The disc, the letters, his death all threads in a single, terrifying weave. And she was now entangled within it.

Their collaboration, once buoyed by shared intellectual excitement, now carried a quiet dread. Elias watched Evelyn more closely these days not as a colleague, but as a fellow traveler on a dangerous path. He noticed the sleepless shadows under her eyes, the subtle tightening of her jaw at any mention of her father, and the flash of defiance that surfaced whenever obstacles rose against her.

He remembered their first meeting at a symposium on ancient cartography. Evelyn, still a graduate student, had stood before a room of esteemed scholars and dismantled a celebrated historian's interpretation of a Ptolemaic map with precision and nerve. He had been captivated then by her clarity of thought and her refusal to yield. That defiance had not dimmed; if anything, it burned hotter now.

Late one night, surrounded by the soft hum of the Lyceum's observation room and the slow rotation of the holographic star chart, Elias finally gave voice to his fear. "Evelyn," he whispered, "I've been troubled. This disc, the texts... they speak of something ancient. Something deliberately hidden." His hand trembled as it gestured toward the cosmic projection. "My faith in the sanctity of knowledge in the belief that all truths must be revealed it's beginning to waver."

Evelyn turned from the glowing cosmos. In his shaken voice, she heard the mirror of her own unease. "I understand," she said softly. "My father used to warn of cursed knowledge. He believed some truths carried a price not just for those who found them, but for everyone around them. He died seeking something like this. And I believe this disc is the key."

The weight of her revelation filled the room like smoke. Elias had known of her father's controversial work but not how deeply it bound her to their current quest. What for him was a philosophical crisis was, for her, a matter of blood and legacy.

He placed a hand gently on her arm. "Evelyn... if this is tied to your father's death, then we must proceed carefully. This isn't just about uncovering history. It's about justice."

Her faint, sorrow-tinged smile carried steel beneath it. "Or about preventing others from sharing his fate. If this gospel reveals what I believe it might, it threatens power itself. And that kind of power is something people are willing to kill for."

The pieces locked together. Elias saw clearly the immense personal weight she carried. His scholarly detachment fractured in that moment, replaced by a shared sense of peril and purpose. He thought of an old Latin phrase he once studied: Lux in tenebris lucet, et tenebrae eam non comprehenderunt. Light shines in the darkness, and the darkness comprehends it not.

Once, he had read it as metaphor. Now, he wondered if it was a warning.

The Lyceum could no longer hold them. The disc was carefully packed away, its leaden weight a constant reminder of what they were walking into. They traveled quietly, blending with a small caravan of antiquarians bound for the lands near Jerusalem. Their faces became just two among many, their purpose masked by feigned interest in pottery and inscriptions.

The air grew drier as they crossed into ochre landscapes, where wind carried the scent of sunbaked stone and the sky burned with relentless light. Villages carved from the earth itself blurred past, and conversations in ancient dialects rolled like distant music.

Evelyn's sharp ear picked up fragments of Aramaic, sharing respectful words with elders who seemed surprised that a foreigner spoke their tongue with fluency. She traced worn olive trees with her fingertips as if drawing strength from the land itself. Elias watched her move through the world as though she were walking in her father's footprints.

At a roadside well, she spotted faint markings etched into weathered stone: spirals and circles echoing the disc's own language. "Look," she whispered. "These are not natural formations." The symbols, though eroded, spoke of rituals long forgotten. Elias felt the past lean close.

Days later, they reached their destination, a ruin buried beneath layers of silence and sand. A skeletal synagogue, its roof long gone, lay half swallowed by the valley. A sagging wall of darker basalt drew Evelyn's attention. She traced the precise seams of the stones, sensing what lay beneath.

Elias found the fracture: a hairline seam in the largest slab. It took their combined effort, careful and deliberate, to pry it open. The stone exhaled centuries of stale air and the faint hum of something electric, something alive.

Within the narrow chamber rested a small pedestal and a single metallic plate. Cool and heavy, it glimmered faintly in the lamplight, its surface etched with geometric patterns unlike any language Elias had encountered. When Evelyn's fingers brushed it, the plate answered with light, soft and pulsing, almost like breath.

"It's not alphabetic," Elias murmured, scanning the strange designs. "It's conceptual. This is a language of forces, not words."

Evelyn nodded, recognizing the swirling forms from her dreams. "A language of the stars," she whispered.

The etched verses spoke of the Great Conjunction, of celestial wine that quenches cosmic thirst, of a veiled summit where truth sleeps. The alignment depicted on the plate was impossibly old, older than recorded civilization. A cosmic event buried beneath time.

They followed the plate's coordinates into mist-wrapped mountains. Their passage grew slower and quieter as the forest thickened. Then came the chanting, low, rhythmic, older than memory. Figures emerged from the trees, moving with practiced grace. Custodians of the mountain.

"You trespass," said the elder. His dialect was ancient, but Elias understood enough.

"We seek knowledge," Elias answered. Evelyn added, "We follow the celestial signs."

The elder studied them with a gaze like bedrock. "The stars guide the chosen or the lost. What you call a gospel is not a gospel. It is a testament. A covenant between the First Ones and the living earth."

He named their plate the Star Seed. A shard of a celestial blueprint left in the First Weaving. A burden and a guide. "The mountain will test you," he warned. "It demands reverence, not conquest."

He gave them glowing stones, the Earth's Song, to hear the mountain's voice. Evelyn felt its warmth seep into her palm like an oath.

As they climbed, the forest changed. Whispers twisted into something sharper. The traps began, the subtle manipulations of terrain, falling stones poised above narrow paths, tripwires of dark, strong fiber hidden beneath the moss.

"They're not here to talk," Evelyn muttered, cutting the wire from Elias's boot.

This was no random interference. Someone else hunted the same prize. Worse, they had infiltrated their notes. Evelyn found a single altered translation just enough to twist meaning, to reduce something sacred to something merely technological.

"They're shaping the narrative," Elias whispered. "Trying to control the meaning before we even understand it."

The veiled summit loomed ahead, not only as a destination but as a battleground.

Under the camp's faint lamplight, they spread brittle papyrus and traced ancient constellations. Sirius glimmered at the center of a spiral. "This is a star chart," Elias said. "But not from our time. This is the sky thousands of years ago."

The calculations pointed to the early Bronze Age; a meteor shower recorded in Egyptian and Mesopotamian texts as the Tears of Anu. Evelyn felt a chill. A celestial event, mapped in scripture, aligned with their fragment.

"These weren't just observers," she said. "They were chroniclers of a cosmic arrival."

The Gospel was not only a text but a star map, a story of celestial shepherds and mountains that touched the sky. Elias matched it with the current night sky, plotting the constellation's shift through precession. The mountain they approached lay directly beneath the alignment that had burned across the heaven's millennia ago.

"This isn't just history," he said. "It's a marker. A message."

The simulated reconstruction of the night sky, 3200 to 3100 BCE, matched the papyrus exactly. Three stars clustered as three lights. A lake reflecting the heavens. A mountain like a needle through the stars.

Evelyn leaned over the chart, her voice barely above the whisper of the wind. "This wasn't metaphor. It was a map."

The gospel of the Hebrews was not a gospel at all. It was a celestial breadcrumb trail leading across millennia. And now, standing beneath the same stars, Evelyn and Elias were no longer mere scholars. They were trespassers in an ancient conversation between earth and sky.

The mountain waited. The stars remembered. And the game had begun long before either of them was born.

3: The Serpent's Coil

The revelation that the celestial map, painstakingly deciphered from the fragile papyrus, pointed not to some distant undiscovered land but to the very heart of Western civilization sent a tremor of anticipation through Evelyn. Rome. The Eternal City, a vast palimpsest of empires, religions, and secrets, was now the nexus of their investigation. The early Bronze Age alignment, the Tears of Anu, the Star Shepherds, all these disparate threads seemed to converge on a single, formidable location.

"Rome," Elias echoed her unspoken thought, his gaze distant, already lost in the architectural and historical complexities of the city. "It makes a terrifying kind of sense. If the Star Shepherds, or those who chronicled their arrival, wished to preserve their knowledge, where better than a place where knowledge has been systematically collected, curated, and at times fiercely guarded for millennia?"

Their journey from the remote mountains, a descent that felt almost like a retreat from the heavens themselves, had been undertaken with renewed purpose. The vastness of the sky, once their primary canvas, had now shrunk to the confines of libraries, archives, and whispered histories of ancient institutions. The custodians, whose knowledge had guided them to the papyrus, offered only cryptic pronouncements about the enduring power of Rome to both illuminate and conceal. "The city that devours all histories," the elder had intoned, his eyes holding a wisdom that transcended generations, "yet remembers some, selectively."

As their carriage rumbled through the outskirts of Rome, the sheer scale of the city began to assert itself. Ancient aqueducts, skeletal and majestic, marched across the landscape, testaments to an engineering prowess that defied easy explanation. The air itself seemed thick with history, a palpable presence woven from the dust of fallen empires and the prayers of countless faithful. Evelyn felt a familiar tightening in her chest; the thrill of the chase mingled with a prickle of apprehension. Rome was a city that wore its past like a conquering emperor, proud and unyielding. But beneath the grandeur, she suspected lay a more intricate, hidden narrative, one that mirrored the labyrinthine streets themselves.

Elias, ever the pragmatist, was already consulting a series of maps and historical documents, his brow furrowed in concentration. "The primary targets, as we discussed, would be the Vatican archives, of course, but also the older monastic libraries and any collections that predate the major Church councils. The period we're interested in, the early Bronze Age, is far too ancient to have direct textual references in Roman archives. However, if there were later records perhaps astronomical observations, theological interpretations, or guarded accounts of visitors, they would most likely be found within institutions that have maintained continuity of record keeping over centuries."

He tapped a finger on a dense section of the map. "The Collegio Romano houses an incredible astronomical observatory, dating back centuries. While its focus is largely on later periods, the collections are vast and often contain older materials. And then there's the Biblioteca Angelica, one of the oldest public libraries in Europe. The sheer density of historical material within these institutions is overwhelming."

Their initial inquiries were met with polite but firm resistance. Access to the Vatican Secret Archives was not a matter of simple request. It required sponsorship, a verifiable research purpose, and, more often than not, an established reputation that few outsiders possessed. Evelyn, despite her credentials, felt like an interloper, a seeker of forbidden knowledge in a temple of hushed secrets.

"The labyrinth begins," she murmured to Elias as they stood before the imposing facade of the Vatican Library. The weight of history emanating from the stones seemed to press down on them. "How do we even begin to navigate this?"

Elias, however, had a plan. He had contacted a former colleague, a respected historian who had spent years studying ancient astronomical texts and their reception within early Christian thought. Professor Valerius Greco, an elderly Roman with a keen intellect and an encyclopedic knowledge of forgotten lore, had agreed to meet them.

Their meeting took place in a quiet trattoria tucked away in a narrow alley near the Pantheon, the ancient structure a silent witness to the city's layered past. The scent of garlic and roasting meat hung in the air, grounding their celestial theories in earthly pleasures. Professor Greco, a man whose white hair framed a face etched with the wisdom of countless books, listened intently as they explained their findings, their voices hushed and reverent as they spoke of the papyrus and the celestial alignment.

"The Star Shepherds," Greco mused, his eyes twinkling as he took a sip of wine. "A fascinating concept. The early Church fathers were not immune to the allure of the heavens. While their interpretations often aligned with Christian doctrine, the underlying observations and the fascination with celestial phenomena were very much present. Many early Christian communities drew heavily on existing pagan and Jewish traditions, including astronomical symbolism."

He leaned forward, his expression becoming serious. "You speak of ancient libraries and archives. Rome, and the Vatican in particular, is a repository of immense knowledge, but also a fortress of selective preservation. Documents deemed heretical, or inconvenient to established dogma, were often suppressed, hidden, or destroyed. However, in their efforts to refute or recontextualize these heretical ideas, the custodians of orthodoxy often preserved fragments, quotes, or summaries of the very material they sought to condemn. It is in these shadows, in the footnotes of refutation, that you might find your new lead."

Greco's words resonated with Evelyn. The idea of finding evidence not in direct preservation but in the very act of suppression was a compelling one. It meant delving into theological debates, into the writings of those who sought to debunk or discredit alternative narratives.

"We are looking for anything that might connect to a significant celestial event in the distant past," Elias clarified. "Specifically, something that predates documented astronomical records but might have been preserved in later theological or historical contexts. The papyrus suggests a time frame around 3000 to 3500 BCE, linked to a major celestial occurrence. We believe this event may have been interpreted by early cultures as a sign of arrival or significant transformation."

Professor Greco nodded slowly. "The Council of Nicaea in 325 AD, for example, was a pivotal moment for standardizing Christian doctrine. While their primary focus was on Christology, the process of codifying beliefs involved examining and rejecting earlier interpretations. There were countless other smaller councils and synods throughout the early centuries of Christianity, each attempting to consolidate the faith. It is within the records of these debates, particularly those concerning eschatology, cosmogony, and the nature of divine intervention, that you might find echoes of older beliefs."

He then spoke of the Ophite's, a sect known for their reverence of the serpent and their Gnostic beliefs that often-intertwined celestial observations with spiritual narratives. Their writings, though largely suppressed, had been referenced and debated by Church fathers in their efforts to expose and condemn Gnosticism. "The Ophite's," Greco explained, "believed in a cosmic order dictated by celestial cycles and in divine beings who descended from the heavens. Their cosmological charts, though few survive, were said to be remarkably intricate, mapping not just stars, but symbolic pathways and spiritual energies."

"The serpent," Evelyn murmured, the word resonating with their book's title, "The Serpent's Coil."

Greco's gaze sharpened. "Indeed. The serpent, in many ancient cultures, was a symbol of wisdom, of cyclical renewal, and of connection to the divine, often associated with celestial phenomena. If your papyrus depicts a serpent-like stellar configuration, or if it was interpreted through that lens, then delving into Gnostic texts, particularly those of the Ophite's and related groups, would be a logical next step."

He provided them with a list of Church fathers whose writings were known to contain refutations of Gnostic ideas, individuals like Irenaeus, Tertullian, and Epiphanius. He also pointed them towards less public collections, monastic libraries scattered throughout Italy, many of which had historical ties to the Vatican and were known to hold older, sometimes less orthodox, manuscripts. "The Angelica Library," Greco suggested, "is a good starting point. They possess a significant collection of early Christian manuscripts, and their cataloging system can sometimes overlook connections that are only apparent to those with a specific, perhaps unconventional, area of research. Look for commentaries on Genesis, on the Book of Revelation, and on any apocryphal texts that were circulating in the early centuries."

He then offered a more veiled but equally crucial piece of advice. "Be discreet. Rome guards its secrets fiercely. Those who delve too deeply into certain historical or theological matters can attract unwanted attention. The custodians of knowledge are not always benevolent."

Their first foray into the Vatican's hallowed halls was a lesson in patience and bureaucracy. After days of navigating a labyrinth of permit applications and security checks, they were finally granted limited access to a section of the Apostolic Archives. The air within was cool and dry, carrying the faint, musty scent of aging paper and ink. Row upon row of meticulously bound volumes stretched into the dim light, each a testament to centuries of record keeping.

Elias focused his attention on theological treatises and commentaries from the third and fourth centuries, searching for any mention of astronomical events linked to divine origins or significant earthly occurrences. Evelyn, meanwhile, delved into historical records that might have documented the activities of various sects or philosophical schools that existed during the Roman Empire, cross-referencing names and places with the vague geographical hints from the papyrus.

Days blurred into a monotonous cycle of dusty tomes and cryptic cross-references. They found extensive debates on the nature of the heavens, the influence of stars on human affairs, and the interpretation of prophecies. There were mentions of comets and eclipses, often framed as omens or divine judgments, but nothing that clearly linked to the specific celestial alignment they had identified. The Tears of Anu remained an obscure ancient event, its significance buried beneath centuries of theological interpretation.

One afternoon, while poring over a volume attributed to Origen, Evelyn stumbled upon a passage that seemed to flicker with relevance. Origen, in his attempt to refute a particular Gnostic interpretation of creation, cited a passage from an unnamed source, a text he referred to as the Chronicle of the Sky Watchers. He used it to highlight what he considered the Gnostics' erroneous beliefs about a cosmic progenitor who arrived from the stars during a specific astronomical configuration.

"Elias," Evelyn whispered, her voice tight with excitement. "Listen to this." She read aloud the translated passage, her finger tracing the ancient Latin script. Origen described how the Chronicle spoke of a time "when the Great Eye, Sirius, rested above the Mountain of the Dawn, and the Serpent of the Heavens coiled around the Pole Star, a celestial ballet that heralded the coming of the First Ones."

Elias's head snapped up, his eyes wide. "The Great Eye, Sirius. The Mountain of the Dawn is a metaphorical reference to the East where the stars rise. And the Serpent of the Heavens... it's a direct parallel to the serpent imagery we've seen. But the timing, Evelyn, the timing is key."

They immediately began searching for any mention of the Chronicle of the Sky Watchers in other texts, hoping for more direct references. Their efforts were met with frustration. Origen's citation was frustratingly isolated, a single tantalizing echo in a vast ocean of theological discourse.

Professor Greco confirmed their suspicions. "Origen was known for his extensive use of esoteric sources, many of which he himself introduced to the scholarly world. The Chronicle of the Sky Watchers is not a known surviving text. It is highly probable that it was a unique manuscript, possibly of Gnostic origin, that was either lost or deliberately destroyed after Origen referenced it in his polemic."

He looked at them thoughtfully. "However, this is precisely the kind of material that would have been preserved, even if only in citations. If Origen used it to refute Gnosticism, then it likely contained ideas that were considered dangerous. The Ophite's, as I mentioned, were deeply involved with Gnostic cosmology and celestial symbolism. It is within their circles that you might find a clearer understanding of this Chronicle and the event it described."

Their focus now shifted to the Bibliotheca Angelica and the less accessible monastic collections. The Angelica, with its labyrinthine stacks, proved to be a treasure trove of theological debate. Evelyn spent hours poring over works that criticized Gnostic sects, looking for any descriptive passages that might allude to the Chronicle or the specific astronomical event.

She discovered that many early Christian writers, in their efforts to debunk Gnostic beliefs, inadvertently provided vivid descriptions of the very ideas they were trying to suppress. They spoke of Gnostic cosmologies that involved a divine descent during stellar alignments, of ancient texts that mapped the heavens and correlated them with spiritual journeys. The serpent imagery was prevalent, often interpreted as a symbol of wisdom, of cyclical times, or of a primordial cosmic force.

One afternoon, buried deep within a collection of fragments attributed to Saint Jerome, Evelyn found a reference that sent a jolt of recognition through her. Jerome, in his polemic against the Ophite's, mentioned their veneration of a "Serpent Star" that guided their ancient ancestors to Earth. He derided their belief that this star was not merely a celestial body but a sentient entity, a guide that appeared during a specific cosmic configuration.

"Elias, look at this," Evelyn said, her voice trembling slightly. She showed him the passage. Jerome wrote, "These Ophite's, in their folly, claim to follow the wisdom of the Serpent, believing that its celestial manifestation, a star that blazed with an unusual light in the days of the ancient ones, guided their lineage to this world. They speak of a time when the heavens themselves rearranged their patterns to welcome their progenitors."

"This is it," Elias breathed, scanning the text with fervent intensity. "The Serpent Star, the celestial manifestation. It's the same narrative, just presented through the lens of critique. Jerome is describing the same event as Origen, and likely referencing the same source, or at least similar traditions."

Their research became more targeted. They began to look for any mention of specific astronomical events tied to the origins of humanity or the arrival of divine beings within writings that criticized Gnostic beliefs. The assumption was that if a Gnostic text spoke of such an event, the Christian writers trying to discredit it would describe it in enough detail for it to be identifiable.

The Angelica Library's collection of manuscripts from Saint Clement of Alexandria proved particularly fruitful. Clement, a scholar who attempted to bridge Hellenistic philosophy with Christian theology, often referenced various schools of thought, including Gnosticism. In his Stromata, he quoted extensively from a variety of sources, often without explicitly naming them but providing enough context for later scholars to identify their likely origins.

Evelyn found a passage where Clement discussed the Gnostic concept of pleroma, the fullness of the divine realm and their belief in emanations from the divine. He then spoke of ancient traditions that charted the cycles of the cosmos and marked auspicious moments for divine incursions into the material world. He mentioned a specific period when, according to "certain ancient reckonings," the celestial bodies aligned in a unique configuration, signifying a time of great change and spiritual transference. He referred to it as the "Season of the Great Descent."

"The Season of the Great Descent," Elias repeated, scribbling furiously in his notebook. "It's not a precise astronomical term, but it aligns with the idea of arrival, of coming from above. And 'ancient reckonings' suggests a record that predates even Clement's time."

Their search had led them into the intellectual battlegrounds of early Christianity. The texts that sought to condemn and eradicate alternative beliefs were now their most valuable sources of information. The Roman libraries and the Vatican archives, once seen as repositories of pure truth, were revealing themselves as complex archives of intellectual struggle, where ideas were debated, suppressed, and inadvertently preserved.

The weight of the Vatican's history began to feel less like a backdrop and more like an active participant in their investigation. They were delving into the very foundations of Western religious thought, unearthing echoes of a past that powerful institutions had tried to bury. The serpent had coiled itself around the very heart of Rome.

Their initial steps into the Vatican's labyrinthine corridors were an exercise in controlled frustration. Elias's academic credentials, while impeccable, were merely a key to the outer gates. The inner sanctum, the repository of the Church's most closely guarded secrets, demanded more. It required a specific, demonstrable research interest that resonated with the Curia, a delicate dance of inquiry and discretion. Evelyn, sensing the bureaucratic walls being erected, employed subtle charm and earnestness, framing their research not as an investigation into esoteric origins, but as a scholarly pursuit to illuminate the intellectual currents of early Christian thought.

The request for access to specific sections of the Apostolic Archives was met with polite, but protracted, deliberation. Days turned into weeks, filled with formal letters, follow-up calls, and increasingly complex questionnaires. The hushed halls of the Vatican Library, where they spent their waiting hours poring over publicly accessible texts, seemed to mock their efforts. Sunlight, filtering through the high arched windows, illuminated dust motes dancing in the air, each particle a silent testament to the slow pace of institutional memory.

Elias confided his concerns during one of their clandestine meetings in a secluded piazza, the scent of cypress trees a sharp contrast to the musty air of their research. "It's not just about finding the documents, Evelyn. It's about being allowed to find them. The systems here are designed to channel inquiry along approved paths. Anything that deviates, anything that hints at an alternative narrative to the one constructed over millennia, is likely to be met with resistance, or worse, redirection."

Their hope rested on Professor Greco's connections. The venerable historian, a scholar of no small repute, hinted at a discreet intermediary, an archivist within the Vatican who possessed an appreciation for unconventional pursuits. The meeting with this intermediary, Father Matteo Rossi, was arranged with the utmost secrecy, in a quiet cloister garden, far from the scrutinizing eyes of the main administrative buildings.

Father Rossi was a man of unassuming presence, his clerical robes blending with the muted tones of the garden. His eyes held a sharp, intelligent gleam, and his hands, though gnarled with age, moved with surprising nimbleness as he unwrapped a small leather-bound parcel. "Professor Greco speaks highly of your work," he began, his voice low. "He mentioned your interest in early astronomical interpretations and their impact on nascent theological frameworks. A fascinating, if challenging, field."

He offered them a subtle smile. "The Archives are not merely a collection of books, but a living organism, with its own rhythms and guardians. Access is granted not by right, but by trust. And trust, as you may have gathered, is not easily earned." He then presented them with a set of coded instructions, a series of obscure references to specific theological commentaries and allegorical interpretations. "These," he explained, "are not the primary documents you seek, but breadcrumbs, leading to the custodians of more sensitive materials. Focus your inquiries on the refutations of Gnostic cosmology, particularly those that touch upon celestial phenomena and primeval origins. The more you engage with the narratives of suppression, the more likely you are to be guided toward the sources of that suppression."

He also provided them with a small, intricately carved wooden token. "This," he said, placing it in Evelyn's hand, "is a symbol of scholarly pursuit recognized by certain collectors of rare knowledge within these walls. Should you find yourself in need of discreet consultation, present this to a member of the Bibliotheca Angelica's senior staff. It may open doors that remain otherwise sealed."

Armed with Father Rossi's veiled guidance, their approach to the Vatican Secret Archives became more strategic. They focused their initial requests on specific theological works. Elias, with his knowledge of theological history, meticulously crafted his research proposal, emphasizing the need to understand the historical context of Gnostic cosmology as it was debated by early Church fathers. Evelyn, meanwhile, leveraged her persuasive skills to highlight the broader academic significance of understanding these intellectual battles in shaping Western thought.

The process of gaining entry to the restricted sections of the Apostolic Archives was a testament to the Vatican's intricate bureaucracy. When they were finally ushered into the hushed expanse of the main reading room, the sheer scale of the collection was overwhelming. The air, cool and still, carried the scent of aged paper, leather, and something indefinably ancient. Towering shelves of dark, polished wood reached toward the vaulted ceilings, disappearing into the semi-darkness. Sunlight, diffused through stained glass depicting saints and biblical scenes, cast muted colors across the polished stone floor.

Here, amidst the silent testament of centuries of accumulated knowledge, they began their deeper dive. Elias examined volumes of patristic writings, searching for subtle allusions, fragmented quotes from suppressed texts preserved within works designed to refute them. Evelyn scoured historical records of early Christian communities and councils, seeking mentions of astronomical interpretations of religious events or ancient lore deemed heretical.

It was during these sessions that Elias found, in a voluminous critique of Marcionism by Tertullian, a passage where the author meticulously dismantled what he described as Marcionite distortions of biblical cosmology. In his zeal to condemn, Tertullian quoted passages that spoke of a celestial hierarchy and a divine presence manifested during specific cosmic alignments. One section described an early Christian sect that believed in a celestial serpent-like entity, a guide accompanying a divine being during a significant event in primeval times.

"This," Elias whispered, pointing to the text, "is describing a celestial phenomenon and linking it to a group that worshipped a serpent symbol. He dismisses it as Gnostic fabrication, but the description itself... it's consistent with what our papyrus suggests."

Evelyn found corroborating references in the acta of a minor synod from the late third century, which condemned certain groups who "worshipped the stars as divine emanations and believed that a great celestial serpent dictated the cycles of existence, heralding the arrival of the Primordial Father." The language sent a shiver down her spine. Another echo, another fragment.

The wooden token proved it's worth when they moved their research to the Bibliotheca Angelica. Presenting it to the head librarian, Dr. Moretti, elicited a subtle nod of recognition. With a hint of reluctance, he granted them access to a private collection of manuscripts not listed in the public catalog. It was within this dimly lit room, thick with the scent of aged vellum and cedarwood, that Evelyn found what she believed to be their most significant breakthrough yet.

Among apocryphal texts and theological commentaries, she discovered marginalia in the hand of a seventeenth-century scholar appended to a rare edition of Irenaeus's Adversus Haereses. The annotations spoke of a lost work referred to as the Astrum Serpentis Liber, the Book of the Serpent Star. The notes described a celestial event in the distant past when a specific configuration of stars, resembling a coiled serpent, appeared in the night sky, heralding a great transformation and the arrival of divine beings.

"Elias, look at this!" Evelyn's voice was barely a whisper. "The Astrum Serpentis Liber. The Book of the Serpent Star. It's exactly what we've been searching for."

Elias leaned closer, his breath catching. "The Great Year... a concept found in ancient Babylonian and Greek astronomy, a long cycle after which celestial bodies return to their original positions. It aligns perfectly with the idea of an ancient cyclical event."

Their investigation had led them to the precipice of a hidden history, deliberately obscured within the very archives that sought to preserve it. The hushed halls of the Vatican were now fertile ground for unearthing the secrets they sought, though through complex and often circuitous routes. The weight of centuries of knowledge and the power of those who controlled it was a constant presence, a reminder of the risks involved in their pursuit.

What they could not know yet was that the serpent's coil they had been tracing through texts and forgotten cosmologies had already begun to tighten around them in the present. And Rome, a city that remembered everything it chose to, was watching.

4: The Alexandria Connection

The rumble of the ferry's engine was a low thrum beneath their feet, a stark contrast to the hushed intensity of Rome. Cyprus, rising from the cerulean embrace of the Mediterranean, offered a different kind of sanctuary. It was a place steeped in history, a crossroads of cultures where Phoenicians, Greeks, Romans, and Byzantines had all left their indelible mark. For Elias and Evelyn, it represented a chance to breathe, to sift through the fragments of their Roman discoveries without the immediate, oppressive weight of unseen eyes. They had left Rome with a gnawing unease, the discovery of the Gospel of the Hebrews and its subsequent suppression now framed by the very real threat of those determined to keep it hidden. Cyprus, with its ancient ports and layered past, felt like a logical next step. Perhaps a forgotten trade route, a less obvious channel of dissemination, had carried this forbidden text, or others like it, across the sea.

Their first destination was Paphos, the ancient capital of Cyprus, a city whose ruins whispered of a vibrant past. Wandering through the preserved mosaics of the House of Dionysus, Evelyn felt a sense of detachment from the danger they had fled. The intricate tessellations, depicting scenes of myth and daily life, were a testament to a civilization that had once thrived here, absorbing and adapting influences from across the known world. She imagined merchants who had walked these very floors, their ships laden with goods from Egypt, Syria, and Greece, their conversations a tapestry of languages and trade agreements. Could such a nexus of commerce have served as a conduit for religious ideas, whispered heresies, and burgeoning faiths?

"Look at this, Elias," Evelyn said, pointing to a section of mosaic depicting a seafaring vessel. "The sails and hull show sophisticated shipbuilding, capable of long voyages. It's easy to imagine these ships carrying not just pottery and textiles, but scrolls, religious texts, ideas passed from one culture to another."

Elias, ever the scholar, examined the architectural remnants of a nearby basilica, its once-grand columns weathered by centuries of sun and sea. "Indeed. Paphos was a major Roman administrative and commercial center. If a text like the Gospel of the Hebrews was circulated discreetly, a prosperous and well-connected port like this would have been ideal. Information, like any other commodity, moved along these routes."

They spent days exploring the archaeological sites, piecing together the historical landscape of the island. At Kourion, the Greco-Roman theatre perched on a cliff offered a dramatic vista of the glittering sea. Evelyn imagined the crowds that had once gathered there, their entertainment a blend of Greek tragedy and Roman spectacle. Remnants of early Christian basilicas stood atop older pagan foundations, a clear testament to the island's religious evolution. Each stone was a silent witness to the ebb and flow of belief systems.

"It's fascinating how seamlessly the religious currents flowed," Elias observed, running his hand over a worn inscription on a fallen capital. "The early Christians here, just as in Rome and Alexandria, operated within a polytheistic framework before transitioning to a state-sanctioned faith. The island's strategic position meant it was constantly exposed to new ideas. A text with a nuanced or unorthodox interpretation of Christ's teachings might have found fertile ground here before suppression became widespread."

Evelyn nodded, recalling the Syriac bishop's vehement condemnations. The bishop had railed against the Gospel of the Hebrews as an affront to established doctrine, a corruption of sacred truth. But what if that corruption was simply a reflection of a competing truth, a branch of early Christianity that had been pruned? Cyprus, with its history as a melting pot, might have been a place where such branches flourished briefly before orthodoxy hardened.

Their inquiries were cautious. They spoke with local historians, archaeologists, and scholars, framing their questions around the dissemination of early Christian literature in the Eastern Mediterranean, the routes through which apocryphal texts might have moved, and the religious climate of Cyprus during the second and third centuries. They were careful not to reveal their true focus.

One afternoon, in a small archive in Limassol, Evelyn stumbled upon a curious entry. It detailed a shipment from Alexandria to Kourion in the late second century. Among the usual commodities, grain, papyrus, and dyes, was a mention of "parchments, bound with linen, for scholarly discourse." The description was vague, likely deliberate.

"Elias, you need to see this," Evelyn whispered, her voice tinged with excitement. "Alexandria to Kourion. 'Parchments for scholarly discourse.' This could be it, a tangible record of texts moving between two crucial centers of early Christianity."

Elias examined the entry, his eyes gleaming. "Alexandria was an intellectual hub, home to the Great Library and a thriving Christian community. Kourion, a Roman city with growing Christian influence, fits the pattern. And 'scholarly discourse' suggests not just personal copies but an exchange of ideas, perhaps theological treatises or foundational texts."

The implication was clear: if Alexandria was a source and Kourion a distribution point, then Cyprus might have been a place where these texts were received, copied, studied, or adapted. The island's relative peace and its position at the crossroads of trade could have allowed such activities to flourish.

They dug deeper, cross-referencing manifests, duties, and local edicts. Though no further direct mentions appeared, they found evidence of a flourishing scriptorium culture in Cypriot cities. There were records of scholars traveling between

Alexandria and Cyprus, indicating an active intellectual exchange.

"It's not definitive proof," Elias admitted later at a café overlooking Paphos harbor. "But it's a strong circumstantial connection. If the Gospel of the Hebrews gained traction in Alexandria, a route through Cyprus is entirely plausible."

Cyprus offered a breathing space, a chance to reassess. The island's history, so entwined with the currents that carried early Christianity across the ancient world, offered a more tangible path.

"Think about it," Evelyn mused. "The bishop who condemned the gospel operated in a region with ties to the East and to trade routes through Cyprus. A copy of the gospel or knowledge of it which could easily have reached here, been studied, and then drawn the attention of those who sought its suppression."

Their time on the island, though brief, yielded a promising lead. The vague mention of "parchments for scholarly discourse" whispered of a more complex and interconnected early Christian landscape than standard histories suggested. The Serpent's Coil, they suspected, had tendrils even here, constricting and controlling the flow of knowledge.

The scent of brine and ancient parchment followed them through the sunlit streets of Larnaca. Their inquiries in Paphos and Kourion had produced tantalizing fragments, but the deeper they dug, the clearer it became that Cyprus was a waypoint, not the source. The faint trail pointed toward Alexandria.

Their investigation led them to a monastery on the island's eastern coast; a cluster of weathered stone buildings steeped in centuries of prayer and scholarship. The Abbot, initially cautious, softened as Elias presented their academic credentials and Evelyn showed genuine fascination with the scriptorium. The library was a labyrinth of vaulted ceilings and alcoves, its shelves heavy with codices and scrolls. The air was thick with the scent of vellum and beeswax.

While examining a catalog compiled centuries earlier, Evelyn noticed an anomaly. Nestled between entries of monastic chronicles and hagiographies was a hurried notation: a consignment of scrolls from the Levant, their origin listed as "Alexandria."

"Elias, look," Evelyn whispered, tracing the faded inscription. "'Parchments from the great storehouse, bound for scholarly discourse.' It's the same phrasing we found in Limassol, but this time with an explicit origin."

Elias leaned closer, recognizing the significance. A monastery in Cyprus acquiring texts directly from Alexandria, the great storehouse of knowledge, was not merely an archival footnote. It was a link in the chain.

"The 'great storehouse' speaks of Alexandria not just as a city," Elias said, "but as a hub. This monastery was clearly part of that network of intellectual exchange."

The entry suggested that Alexandria's vast collections were a source for scholarly material, possibly including the Gospel of the Hebrews. Alexandria, with its intellectual melting pot, would have been the perfect environment for preservation, study, and perhaps reinterpretation.

"If Alexandria was the source," Evelyn said, "and this monastery the recipient, then these texts were valued. They weren't luxury goods; they were meant to be studied and debated."

The Abbot, sensing their growing excitement, granted further access. He guided them to a small chamber housing texts too fragile for the main collection. Wrapped in linen within a wooden box were fragments of papyrus bearing Aramaic script. The presence of Aramaic texts in a Cypriot monastery, likely acquired through trade routes from regions where Aramaic was spoken, further corroborated the existence of a wide linguistic and cultural exchange.

"This is extraordinary," Elias murmured. "Aramaic script. It links directly to the Palestinian origins of Christianity. If such texts were traded and studied in Alexandria, and then brought here, it paints a far more interconnected picture of early Christianity than we're often led to believe."

He thought of the bishops who had condemned the Gospel of the Hebrews, their fervent declarations of its corruption. What if these "foreign influences" were not corruptions but alternative expressions of early faith, preserved in centers like Alexandria?

The Abbot, with a knowing look, presented them with a scroll. "This," he said softly, "records texts brought here for copying in the late second century." Near the end of the scroll was a single line: "Scrolls from the Library, for translation and commentary."

The Library. It could only mean the Great Library of Alexandria. The fact that texts from that legendary institution had been brought to Cyprus confirmed their hypothesis: Alexandria was the nexus. Cyprus was a facilitator. The whispers from across the sea were louder now, urging them toward the source.

Alexandria. The name itself was a siren song to any scholar of the ancient world. It conjured images of towering scrolls, ceaseless debate, and the birthplace of many intellectual traditions. The Alexandria they sought was not just the vibrant city of Ptolemaic and Roman Egypt, but a crucible where faith was debated and codified. Their pursuit of the Gospel of the Hebrews was no longer a textual excavation but an immersion in the currents that had shaped Christianity itself.

Evelyn felt anticipation as they arranged passage on a merchant vessel bound for Egypt. Elias, pragmatic as ever, understood that Alexandria was not merely a library but a bustling port where intellectual and commercial currents intertwined. Texts could be hidden in plain sight, traveling with trade goods to avoid detection.

The Great Library's destruction had become legend, a tapestry of fires, decrees, and sectarian strife. But Evelyn and Elias saw its decline not as an end but as a dispersal. Knowledge rarely vanishes entirely. It flows like a river, carving new channels.

"Think of the scholars who worked there," Elias said as the ship left Cyprus behind. "Men like Hypatia. They would not let their texts perish. They would have preserved and disseminated them."

Evelyn imagined those scholars, their intellectual fervor, and the communities who might have safeguarded unorthodox writings. She thought of texts hidden in private libraries, spirited to monasteries, or copied into oblivion by sympathetic scribes.

The destruction of the Library was gradual a series of erosions across centuries. Yet its legacy persisted in the scholars it trained and the texts they carried forward. Christianization had shifted the locus of textual preservation into new hands: monasteries, scriptoriums, and theological schools. These institutions, even as orthodoxy solidified, often preserved older knowledge out of habit, scholarship, or quiet defiance.

Elias pointed out the role of the Mouseion, the research institute linked to the Library. This was more than a repository; it was a crucible where texts were translated, annotated, and debated. The Gospel of the Hebrews, with its potentially radical interpretation, would have drawn attention.

"Even if they opposed it," Elias said, "they would have preserved it to refute it."

The decline of the Library was not erasure but dispersal. Religious communities, especially monasteries, inherited this intellectual legacy. The Cyprus monastery they had just visited stood as proof. These were deliberate acquisitions, purposeful acts of scholarship.

Alexandria's trade networks provided the perfect means of transmission. Scrolls could travel with papyrus, wine, or textiles. What emerged was not destruction but transformation, a dispersal of seeds that sprouted in scattered monastic outposts.

But their journey was not without unease. A pattern of obstruction emerged as soon as they began inquiries in Alexandria. A polite but firm letter informed Elias that the documents he sought had been destroyed in a "tragic fire." A meeting with a respected Coptic scholar was abruptly canceled due to a sudden illness, though he had been healthy days earlier. Attempts to contact him were met by guarded silence.

Their scholarly network began to fray. Subtle misfortunes and delays accumulated like stones in a river, redirecting their efforts. A merchant with an early Christian collection suffered a mysterious "plumbing leak" the night before Evelyn's visit. Elias smelled burnt parchment at a record office that claimed to be "under cataloging review." It became clear: someone was quietly watching, quietly intervening.

The paranoia thickened. Every ally was reevaluated. Every helpful gesture weighed. It was a war fought not with blades but with misdirection and silence. If they wanted the truth, they would have to become as adept at surviving as they were at reading ancient scripts.

As the sun set over Alexandria's harbor, painting the sea in ochre and vermilion, Evelyn and Elias stood on the deck of their ship, the scent of spices mingling with brine. The city rose from the water like a living manuscript, its layers waiting to be read. Their journey, guided by whispers from Rome and Cyprus, had brought them to the heart of a world that had once shaped everything they now sought to uncover.

The fragments unearthed on Cyprus carried a language of symbols. These were not straightforward declarations but intricate metaphors and cryptic sigils that resonated with Gnostic thought. Elias recognized motifs common in Alexandrian philosophical circles, a stylized eye within a triangle, a symbol of spiritual illumination.

"This isn't decoration," Elias explained. "It speaks of direct apprehension of the divine, the hallmark of those who sought understanding through inner illumination."

Evelyn's training in theology and symbolism came alive. She recalled the Valentinian school and its cosmology of emanations, light, and hidden truths. The Gospel of the Hebrews might not have been a single fixed text but a collection of teachings shaped by various groups. In Alexandria, where Jewish mysticism, Platonic philosophy, nascent Christian theology, and Gnostic speculation converged, this made perfect sense.

Alexandrian scholars were renowned for dissecting texts, not merely preserving them. Within this charged environment, the Gospel of the Hebrews could have been preserved, debated, and disseminated, its subversive teachings veiled in symbolic language accessible only to initiates.

"Consider the early Christian communities here," Evelyn said. "Ebionites, Hellenistic believers, Gnostics. All these groups could have drawn from this text, each interpreting it through their own lens."

Elias nodded, eyes on the lighthouse beyond the harbor. "The serpent, the river, the tree, these symbols are more than imagery. They're maps. Gnostic thought is layered. A serpent coiled around a tree often represents wisdom descending into the world, not temptation."

Evelyn thought of the references to the "hidden spring," a source of divine knowledge within the city. Perhaps it pointed to a real enclave, a community guarding such texts.

Elias cross-referenced these symbols with known sites, the Serapeum, the Caesareum, the philosophical schools, the early basilicas. Evelyn focused on the Gnostic dualism of light and darkness. The text's references to "the dawn breaking through the veil of night" aligned with the Gnostic view of light as revelation and darkness as spiritual ignorance.

"The language is sophisticated," Elias observed. "These weren't peasant tracts. They circulated among scholars, philosophers, and theologians."

Figures like Clement of Alexandria had engaged deeply with Gnostic and philosophical traditions, sometimes refuting them, sometimes absorbing them. This engagement, even adversarial, ensured preservation in some form.

Evelyn saw the symbols not as passive decoration but as active communication. Each pattern, each number, might point to specific schools or teachers.

Their pursuit was no longer just a hunt for a lost text, it was the reconstruction of an intellectual lineage. Every symbol was a marker left by someone who had navigated this current centuries before them. Alexandria was not merely a destination. It was the key.

The city loomed ahead, not as a relic but as a living repository of knowledge. Its layered past, both glorious and dangerous, beckoned them into the symbolic heart of a faith older and more contested than the world wanted to remember.

5: The Sands of Time

The air in Alexandria was thick and heavy, not just with the tang of salt and sea, but with the suffocating weight of heat. It clung to Evelyn and Elias like a shroud as they disembarked, the shimmering haze distorting the once grand facades of the harbor into wavering mirages. The city that had promised ancient wisdom now greeted them with a disorienting assault on the senses. The shouting of vendors, the bleating of goats, the rumble of cartwheels on uneven stones, and the modern city's restless hum created a dizzying symphony. It was a stark contrast to the quiet, scholarly air of Cyprus. Alexandria was alive, but its vitality was chaotic, unpredictable and overwhelming. It felt like a force of its own, far removed from the measured quiet of libraries and whispered debates.

"It's certainly more vibrant than I'd imagined," Evelyn murmured, pulling her shawl tighter against the relentless sun. Her gaze swept over the bustling quay, a mosaic of colors and faces, a living testament to the city's enduring role as a crossroads of civilizations. The density of bodies and the collision of scents; fruit, fish, sweat and something faintly floral, were nothing like the curated silence of their prior research. Elias, ever the observer, scanned the crowd with a practiced eye. Traders hawked their wares with seasoned intensity. Veiled women moved gracefully through the crush. Soldiers in bright uniforms reminded them of both the city's precarious order and their own.

Beneath the immediacy of the spectacle lay their true purpose. The cryptic fragments unearthed on Cyprus whispered of a lost gospel tied to this very city. Alexandria, once the intellectual jewel of the ancient world, held the scattered remnants of that legacy beneath layers of empire and sand. Their quest was no longer merely academic. Unseen forces had already taken an interest in Cyprus. Here, every shadow might hold a threat. Every glance might be an observation. They were stepping into a labyrinth where history's echoes mingled with modern danger.

Elias steered them away from the most crowded streets. "We need to find a reputable antiquarian," he said quietly. "Someone who can navigate the institutional landscape and point us toward older collections. The Museum of Alexandria is our most logical starting point. It's where the major finds are housed and studied."

Evelyn nodded. Gaining access would require diplomacy, not force. Their work touched on subjects many considered sensitive. Drawing attention could be dangerous.

The journey to the Museum was a baptism by fire. They hired a caleche driven by a man whose eyes had seen too much sun. The ride was jarring, the carriage bouncing over fractured roads. The grandeur of Roman Alexandria clashed with utilitarian buildings and ruins half swallowed by time. Crumbling mosaics peeked through dust, silent witnesses to the city's layered past.

Evelyn's unease grew as she scanned the edges of the street. Men lingered too long near stalls. Uniformed officials watched the flow of people. Elias noticed it too. They were no longer anonymous travelers. They were being observed.

The Museum loomed ahead, its classical architecture a poignant echo of the city's intellectual heritage. As they stepped inside, the cool marble halls gave them momentary relief. But the silence here was unlike the quiet of Cyprus. It held the weight of history.

Their first contact was Dr. Elara Hassan, a curator with sharp intellect and no patience for posturing. Her immaculate office contrasted sharply with the chaos outside. Evelyn, taking the lead, presented their credentials and framed their inquiry as a scholarly study of early Christian textual traditions. Elias added citations and historical precedents, careful to keep the esoteric implications of their search hidden.

Dr. Hassan listened intently, her fingers steepled. "Alexandria's history is a complex tapestry," she began. "The Great Library is gone. What remains are fragments scattered across collections, some here, some in private hands, many lost to neglect. The Gospel of the Hebrews is intriguing but not something that leaps out from our catalogs. If it exists, it will likely survive through indirect references, citations and commentary."

Evelyn met her gaze steadily. "Our research in Cyprus indicated textual traditions influential in this region. We're interested in papyri, codices or marginalia tied to early Jewish Christian thought, particularly interpretations that predate or run alongside more Hellenized versions."

"Jewish Christian dialogue was vibrant here," Dr. Hassan mused. "Some sought to maintain Jewish roots. Others embraced Hellenistic philosophy. Gnostic movements thrived. Texts were translated, adapted and debated. To find what you seek, you must trace the intellectual echoes rather than the original manuscript. It's like finding a grain of sand on a vast beach."

Elias leaned forward. "We're not expecting a single pristine text. We're searching for the currents, the annotations, the influence, the symbolic frameworks we've already seen on Cyprus."

Recognition flickered in Dr. Hassan's eyes. "Symbolism was a hallmark of Alexandrian schools, especially Gnostic and proto-Gnostic traditions. If such a text existed, its presence would be felt through influence, for example in references in Clement of Alexandria's writings. He refuted heterodox ideas but preserved fragments of them in doing so."

She outlined the reality of their task. Ancient collections had been fragmented by centuries of upheaval, fragile papyri lost or deliberately purged. Yet some fragments survived in the remnants of the Serapeum, in private archives bequeathed to the Museum, in burial sites. "Your best hope," she concluded, "is in commentary sections. Look for deviations, symbolic language, unusual terminology. We can grant you archive access. But this will require time, patience and diligence."

As they left her office, the magnitude of their search weighed on them. But beneath it was a spark of excitement. Alexandria held keys. The Museum was their gateway.

The archives were labyrinthine, a hushed maze of boxes, shelves and fragile memory. Papyri browned with age lay in acid free containers. Codices rested in controlled climates. The air smelled faintly of paper and chemicals, far from the heat and dust outside.

Evelyn and Elias moved methodically. They scanned catalog entries, cross referencing Cyprus with the archive's holdings. They sought the subtle: marginalia, apocryphal references, theological commentaries on texts long lost.

Their breakthrough came slowly. A collection of papyrus fragments from a Roman villa in Canopic caught Evelyn's attention. Officially labeled "miscellaneous administrative and literary fragments," they contained annotations in a flowing Greek hand. These were not mere corrections. They were symbolic, allegorical interpretations.

"Elias," she whispered, tracing the ink. "The passage about the loaves and fishes. Look. It's not about bread. It's about knowledge. The loaves are the five books of Moses. The fish, perhaps the prophetic and the law. The twelve baskets, the tribes."

He leaned in. "The scribe isn't copying. He's interpreting. A guardian of meaning."

The villa site became their new focus. Excavation records were sparse. Much had been rushed into storage to make way for modern development. But their scholarly persistence earned them access to the neglected storerooms.

There, among broken pottery and faded mosaics, they unearthed the real treasure. Carved stone seals, coiled serpents, lotus blossoms and watchful eyes were etched into polished surfaces. Evelyn arranged them on velvet. "They form a sequence," she said. "The serpent motif repeats, always with specific Greek letters. It's a code."

Elias examined a fragment of papyrus beside the seals. "They're marking texts. An encoded library."

The villa was no ordinary house. It was a hidden scriptorium, a place where texts were copied and cloaked in symbols. The seals were keys. Fragments of maps and astronomical observations hinted at deliberate preservation for future hands.

Elias unrolled a vellum scroll of exceptional quality. A brief note, written in a different hand, leapt from the page: "The tradition of the Hebrews, as passed down from Yeshua the Nazarene, is herein preserved for the initiates. Let the Serpent guide you through the celestial spheres, and the Lotus bloom within your spirit."

"This is it," he breathed. "The tradition of the Hebrews. The serpent and the lotus are in the text."

The scroll was part of a cache hidden beneath the villa's floor, protected by lead and bitumen. Inside were preserved papyri describing Matthew's dialogues with Jewish scribes and Mary Magdalene's role as interpreter of inner teachings. A codex of luminous vellum bore a serpent embossed leather cover. The script, a fusion of Greek and Hebrew, read simply: The Hebrew Gospel.

It was not a canonical gospel. It was a mosaic of mystical teachings rooted in Jewish thought. It spoke of intention, spiritual rebirth and an inclusive vision of faith. Elias began transliterating. Evelyn traced its symbolism to the Gnostic echoes they had seen before.

But such knowledge had been hidden for a reason. The scriptorium had dispersed its treasures centuries ago to escape suppression. The discovery carried weight, and danger.

Their next step led them out of the city, deep into the Egyptian desert. The vellum map pointed south of the Fayoum Oasis, toward ruins buried by time. Their preparations were precise: water, medical kits and a generator for their scanners. The journey was a battle against dust and heat. The desert felt alive, vast and indifferent.

A sandstorm rose without warning. The wind howled, sand slashing against the vehicle as they huddled behind a crumbling wall. The storm raged for hours, reducing the world to ocher blindness. When it finally broke, their path was buried. But they pressed on, driven by the whisper of history.

The ruins emerged as low mounds and scattered stones. They established a base and began their survey. Elias's ground penetrating radar revealed a network of underground chambers. Their excavation was patient. Pottery and bronze tools gave way to carved symbols. Beneath a collapsed structure they found stone chests sealed with the same serpent and lotus motifs.

Using a pulley rig, they lifted the lids with surgical precision. Inside were codices bound in dark leather, vellum pages dense with Greek and stylized Hebrew. "The serpent guides the seeker," Elias whispered, studying an illuminated page. Evelyn felt a subtle warmth from the binding, as if the text itself breathed.

Among the trove lay a small indigo codex. Its metallic serpent shimmered faintly. The title, The Gospel of the Hidden Path, sent a current through them both. A text whispered about, dismissed by scholars, lay before them, untouched for centuries.

Their triumph was short lived.

The desert wind fell silent. Radios went dead. Elias scanned the horizon. Figures advanced in formation. They were armed, efficient and purposeful. A dozen operatives approached without pretense. Their leader's voice cut through the still air. "Evelyn Hayes. Elias Finch. You have something that does not belong to you."

Elias started the engine, swerving through the sand. The pursuers opened fire. The chase was brutal, carving across dunes and ravines. Elias veered into a narrow canyon. When they were boxed in, he created chaos with a single flare and a burst of fuel. The explosion bought them seconds. He and Evelyn escaped through a narrow crevice as the fire roared behind them.

Gasping in the shadows of a hidden alcove, they understood the truth. This was not an academic disagreement. They were being hunted by a network determined to suppress what they had found.

"They want the codices," Elias said grimly. "And they'll kill for them."

They abandoned their destroyed vehicle and moved deeper into the desert, following the dry lines of an ancient wadi. Evelyn's mind returned to their discoveries. The codices bore hints of something else, a bridge between Hebrew teachings and Coptic traditions. Early Coptic communities had preserved unorthodox texts before, shielding them from Rome's reach.

"The Copts preserved so many apocryphal writings," she said. "What if the Gospel of the Hebrews was among them? Hidden, adapted, but alive."

Elias nodded. "Monastic communities in the desert were perfect custodians. Independent. Resistant."

They found shelter in a cave system marked on an old survey map. Inside, the air was cool and still. The codices glimmered faintly under their lamps. Evelyn brushed dust from a page and found a Coptic inscription intertwined with hieratic symbols, a deliberate weaving of traditions.

"This is it," she whispered. "The Egyptians didn't just preserve the Hebrew teachings. They integrated them. Logos beside Ma'at."

Elias leaned closer. "This confirms it. The Copts were not passive guardians. They were coauthors of a living tradition."

The inscription was a roadmap, a theological bridge between Hebrew mysticism and Egyptian spiritual cosmology. The serpent, the lotus and the word were not symbols of heresy but of synthesis. This was a tradition designed to endure.

The sound of engines broke the stillness. Their pursuers were closing in. Elias scanned the cave for another way out. Evelyn clutched the codices. They had uncovered not just a lost gospel but a suppressed lineage, a spiritual undercurrent stretching back to the first centuries of the faith. And someone intended to bury it once again.

They gathered their equipment and moved toward a narrow tunnel at the back of the cave. The desert beyond was dark, silent and waiting. What they carried was more than parchment and ink. It was the weight of centuries, the echo of voices long silenced. Their journey was no longer about discovery alone. It was about preservation. And survival.

6: The Ethiopian Enigma

The silence of the ravine had been a brief mercy. Now the sun burned down on their backs, the memory of the smoldering vehicle driving them forward. Evelyn's fingers, still gritty from their escape, brushed the cracked leather of the codices. These were not relics. They were living testaments to a history of powerful forces were desperate to bury. The voices of their pursuers had made that clear, their fixation on the Gospel of the Hebrews sharp as a blade. This was no ordinary chase. It was a battle for control of the past.

"They won't stop," Evelyn rasped, the dry air scraping her throat. "The leader's obsession with the gospel proves it contains something they fear, something they have to control."

Elias, steady as always, bent over the crumpled topographical map, the fragile paper, a stark contrast to the brutal landscape. "Vulnerable is an understatement," he said, scanning the horizon. "They'll comb the ravine inch by inch. We need cover, not just a hiding place." His finger traced a faint network of wadies, dry riverbeds snaking through the desert like forgotten veins. "Here. These might give us shelter."

They moved carefully, their boots crunching against broken stone. The weight of their discovery pressed on Evelyn's chest like a second sun. The Gospel of the Hebrews wasn't just an artifact. It was a living thread of thought, a voice their enemies were determined to silence. The whisper had begun in Alexandria, soft but insistent, growing louder with every inscription they deciphered. The Coptic connection, she believed now, was not a footnote but a key.

"Elias," she whispered, "think of the Coptic Church. They preserved what Rome called heresy. The fragments we found... what if the gospel wasn't a single text but a stream of teachings, passed along through Coptic communities?"

Elias kept his eyes on the terrain, guiding their path with quiet precision. "It fits. Coptic monasteries shielded apocryphal gospels from the reach of the Church. Isolated, fiercely loyal to their traditions, they would have been perfect guardians."

Evelyn pictured the desert fathers, men who sought divine truth in the wilderness. Their monasteries were libraries of dangerous wisdom. The Coptic language, born of ancient Egyptian, was a vessel that carried old gods and new revelations alike. Perhaps the Hebrew roots of early Christianity had found refuge there, far from the Hellenized power centers of Rome.

"Consider the Gnostic texts," she continued. "Many written in Coptic, many presenting Jesus not as a distant figure of divinity but as a teacher of hidden knowledge. 'Knowing' rather than 'believing.' It mirrors the fragments we found."

Elias offered a hand as she scrambled over loose rock. "And persecution made them experts at hiding. They could encode their scriptures, embed meanings in language and symbols no Roman bishop would understand."

The wadi walls rose high around them, casting cool shadows across the sand. The silence here was older, carved by centuries of wind and worship. Evelyn imagined scribes bent over vellum, their pens shaping the looping letters of Coptic script with patient devotion.

"The word Coptic comes from Aigyptos," she said softly. "But it became more than 'Egyptian.' It meant people who resisted being erased. People who kept their language alive."

She remembered a line from a weathered manuscript: "A Hebrew mother, and wisdom hidden through her line." A maternal image, subversive in a church growing rigidly patriarchal. In Egypt, where older matriarchal traditions still whispered beneath the Christian surface, such words might have endured.

Elias suddenly lifted a hand. "Listen."

A faint engine rumbled through the still air. Their pursuers were closing in.

"There's a cave system ahead," Elias said, voice taut. "We make for it now."

As they pressed deeper into the ravine, Evelyn's thoughts stayed with the Copts. The early Church was no single story but a storm of competing visions. The Council of Nicaea had chosen one narrative, but others had endured, hidden in the margins, kept alive by hands determined to remember. If the Gospel of the Hebrews challenged Rome's claim to divine authority, Coptic Egypt was the perfect place for it to survive.

Elias pointed toward a narrow cleft in the cliff. "There."

They slipped inside. The air cooled instantly, thick with the scent of stone and ancient time. Elias set down the codices on a smooth rock. "We take stock here. And then we read."

Evelyn knelt in the circle of his flashlight, the ancient ink breathing stories through the dust. Her pulse quickened. Somewhere within these fragile pages lay the truth they had risked everything to find. She turned a leaf carefully, revealing a faded inscription.

Symbols intertwined: Coptic letters and an older Egyptian script. A message left by guardians long dead. A map, perhaps. Or a warning.

"Elias," she whispered, "this is it. They didn't just hide the gospel. They wove it into their own tradition."

He leaned in. "And this symbol, Ma'at, truth and balance beside logos. They weren't fighting Rome with swords. They were defending truth with scripture."

The weight of the revelation was staggering. The Gospel of the Hebrews wasn't presented as heresy. It was framed as fulfillment, a bridge between old gods and a new Christ. Evelyn saw the plan for what it was: make the text inseparable from Coptic faith, and Rome could never erase it.

"They anchored it in their own language," she murmured. "Even if Rome won, the gospel would outlast them."

Their examination was cut short by the rising growl of engines outside.

"They've found us," Elias said. "We move deeper."

They gathered the codices and slipped through a narrow passage at the back of the cave. The stone scraped their hands and knees, the tunnel closing in like the throat of the earth. Evelyn could feel history pressing against her as tangibly as the rough stone. She imagined generations of scribes crawling through these same passageways, their torches flickering, their secrets intact.

When they finally emerged, the desert had transformed. The sun was setting, and below the plateau, bathed in amber light, stretched a city of stone stela and ancient power.

"Axum," Elias breathed. "We've found it."

The Ethiopian sun was softer here; its warmth pooled across the plateau as they descended toward the ancient city. Axum rose from the earth like a relic that refused to be forgotten. Stone stela pierced the twilight sky, tall and solemn, their surfaces etched with stories that predated empires. Each obelisk seemed alive, bearing silent witness to centuries of devotion and the ebb of forgotten kingdoms.

Evelyn felt it immediately, that quiet weight of history that made every breath feel reverent. This was not just a city; it was a living archive.

"Axum," Elias whispered, as if speaking too loudly might fracture the moment. "Legends say the Ark rests here. And maybe our gospel with it."

The descent was careful, deliberate. They moved like ghosts among stones. The air carried the faint scent of incense and earth. Evening shadows stretched long across ancient walls. At the center of the city stood the Church of Our Lady Mary of Zion, its silhouette both austere and luminous against the fading light. This was the beating heart of Ethiopian Christianity, a place where myth and memory had fused into something unshakable.

The church complex was a blend of eras: basilica walls, weathered rock-hewn chapels, and gardens that seemed untouched by time. Monks moved like figures from another age, their robes whispering as they passed. Evelyn felt the pull immediately. If the Gospel of the Hebrews had survived anywhere, it would be in a place like this.

Inside, the air thickened with incense, candle wax, and old stone. Frescoes cloaked the walls in fading color, scenes of saints and angels painted by hands long turned to dust. The chanting of monks echoed through the nave, a low, resonant hum that seemed to rise from the very bones of the earth. Evelyn paused in the threshold, feeling the vibration of centuries in her chest.

Elias approached the monks with studied respect. He spoke softly, his words crafted to sound like the inquiries of an academic, not a seeker of forbidden knowledge. They responded with measured politeness, their pride tempered with caution. Outsiders rarely came asking about manuscripts. Outsiders asking the wrong questions were remembered.

Evelyn let her gaze wander. She traced the curvature of old arches, the patterns in the faded paint. Subtle echoes of Coptic design lingered in the corners, brushstrokes that whispered of Alexandria and the Nile. The clues were quiet, but they were here.

Their audience with the elder monks stretched deep into the night. They learned of manuscripts in Ge'ez, the ancient liturgical language of Ethiopia, preserved across centuries by generations of scribes. The monks spoke with reverence, but their words were careful. Some things, Evelyn understood, were not freely given.

One elder, his eyes clouded yet sharp with memory, told them fragments of an older tale: a gospel carried across lands in secret, a text that predated Rome's dominance. His voice was calm but edged with warning. These were stories that did not belong to outsiders.

In the scriptorium, the light was dim, filtered through narrow windows and pools of flickering oil lamps. Evelyn watched the monk's work. Every movement was deliberate. Quills dipped into ink with quiet ritual; vellum smoothed with patient hands. This was a place where time itself had slowed to protect what it held.

Among a stack of weathered commentaries, Evelyn found it: not the gospel itself, but a cipher. Marginal notations in Ge'ez, symbols intertwined with a rhythm she recognized from early Coptic monastic scripts. Hidden in the edges, as if meant for someone who already knew how to look.

"Elias," she whispered, her pulse quickening. "This isn't commentary. It's a code."

He leaned over her shoulder. "It's cleaner than I expected. Whoever wrote this knew how to bury meaning in plain sight."

The cipher was the kind of evidence that changed everything. It wasn't proof, not yet, but it was a signpost, a whisper across centuries from those who had hidden the Gospel of the Hebrews and sworn to keep it safe.

But the monastery was not blind. Their quiet inquiries had stirred ripples. Eyes followed them now, patient and watchful. The air had changed. Trust was fragile here.

Outside, the city breathed with the weight of prophecy. The stela stood like sentinels, and the wind carried old prayers. Evelyn felt the line between faith and danger blur. They were no longer just scholars in search of a text. They were walking into a centuries-old covenant, guarded by men who would not yield it easily.

"Whatever is here," Elias murmured as they stepped into the night, "they've been protecting it for a long time. And someone else knows we're getting close."

Evelyn looked back toward the dark outline of the church. The gospel, if it existed here, was more than a lost manuscript. It was the buried root of a narrative others had spent centuries trying to control.

The hunt was no longer just about history. It was about who was willing to kill to keep it silent.

At first, the resistance came like a change in the wind. Subtle. Quiet. A smile that faltered too quickly. A door that once opened easily now stayed latched, a moment too long. Evelyn felt it before Elias said it aloud.

"Our questions are echoing back at us," he observed one night, seated at the small wooden table in their room above a quiet street. The lamp cast a thin halo across their scattered notes. "Someone's listening."

Evelyn tapped the ciphered symbols she'd copied from the margins of the Ge'ez manuscript. "And someone wants us to stop."

Their guide, Gebre, had been the first to vanish. He was reliable, connected to the monastic networks in the north. Then one morning, his bed was cold, his door ajar, his possessions untouched. Only a single note remained: "The light you chase casts a long shadow."

The script was angular, unfamiliar. Elias recognized the precision. "A mark," he said. "They're not just watching. They're warning."

It was how the organization always moved. Quiet first. Direct only when necessary. They did not need to appear. They only needed to make the air heavier.

Whispers spread through the narrow streets of Axum. Foreigners asking questions about holy texts. Outsiders with dangerous curiosity. By the third day, the shopkeepers who once greeted them with warm bread and cardamom coffee now turned away with polite, rehearsed caution.

"They're turning the city against us," Elias muttered as they crossed the shadow of the great stela. "Classic isolation strategy. Cut us off from trust before we can build it."

Evelyn could feel the unease thickening around them. The monks who once offered patient smiles now watched from cloistered arches with folded arms. The abbot at Debre Damo had cut their meeting short with a carefully worded dismissal. It wasn't hostility. It was fear. Someone had reached him first.

"They've been here," Evelyn whispered as they descended the cliff path. "They poisoned the well long before we arrived."

The organization was a phantom, no single face, no single name. They appeared where history pressed against power.

They didn't destroy texts; they buried them so deep they might as well have never existed.

The cipher Evelyn found became their only anchor. She worked in silence each night, candlelight sharpening the black curves of her ink. It was a layered code: Coptic forms buried in Ge'ez structure, threaded with fragments that echoed something older still. Whoever created it had expected pursuers and left a trail only the initiated could follow.

"It's not just a text," she said quietly as Elias leaned over her work. "It's a map."

He nodded. "And they know we've seen it."

Every move they made in Axum felt observed. A man lingered too long near the church gate. A child, barefoot and silent, carried messages they couldn't read. Doors shut faster when they passed. It was the kind of pressure that didn't need violence. It made the hunted doubt their own footing.

"They're shifting from shadow to presence," Elias said one evening as he packed their notes into the worn satchel. "We don't have long before they close the net."

Evelyn looked at the cipher again. There was no mistaking it now. It pointed toward something buried far from the church, a monastery hidden in the northern highlands.

"Then we go before they do," she said.

That night they left Axum in silence, moving beneath the weight of stars older than the gospel itself. The wind carried the faint scent of dust and incense. Behind them, the stela stood in mute vigil. Ahead, the highlands waited, and with them, the next turn of the hidden trail.

But somewhere in the darkness, another set of footsteps was already moving.

The highlands opened before them like the ribs of the earth, sharp ridges and shadowed valleys folding into one another in a labyrinth of wind and stone. The night air was thin, dry, and alive with a kind of silence that felt older than language. Evelyn walked behind Elias along a goat trail carved centuries earlier, her fingers brushing the cold edge of the ravine wall. Every sound was amplified: a pebble dislodged beneath a boot, the whisper of fabric against rock, the faint rasp of their breath.

The cipher's coordinates had led them here, to a remote plateau where a monastery clung to a cliff like an afterthought of faith. The structure was barely visible in the moonlight, its rough-hewn stone walls blending into the mountain. No road led here. Only narrow switchbacks and the kind of knowledge that is whispered rather than written.

Elias stopped and crouched, scanning the jagged slope below. Two lanterns bobbed faintly along the lower path. Too steady for shepherds. Too late for pilgrims.

"They're following," he said softly.

Evelyn's hand tightened around the strap of the satchel. "Then we're ahead, but not by much."

The ascent to the monastery was brutal, each step cut from centuries of rock and prayer. By the time they reached the outer gate, the horizon was pale with the first light of dawn. An iron bell hung motionless over the entrance, dark with age. No one greeted them.

The monks here lived in deliberate obscurity. No written records, no visitors. The monastery was carved partly into the cliff, its inner chambers accessible only through a single narrow archway that smelled of earth and incense.

An old monk emerged from the shadows. His face was creased like weathered parchment, his eyes clear and piercing. He regarded them in silence for a long time before speaking in slow, deliberate Ge'ez. Elias answered carefully, his tone low, respectful. The exchange was measured, almost ritualistic.

Evelyn understood only fragments of the words but everything in the cadence: this was not a welcome. It was a test.

At last, the monk turned and gestured for them to follow. They passed through a passageway barely wide enough for a single person, the stone walls cold and smooth beneath their fingers. The air grew cooler as they descended, torches flickering in wall niches.

The scriptorium lay underground, carved into the rock like a buried cathedral. Shelves lined the walls, stacked with scrolls bound in leather darkened by centuries. The faint scent of beeswax and parchment hung in the air. Evelyn felt the weight of history settle over her like a second skin.

"This is where they hid it," she whispered.

Elias nodded once. He could feel it too.

The monk stopped before an alcove recessed into the stone. He placed his hand on a carved relief: a winged figure holding a scroll. The wall shifted with a dull, ancient sound. Behind it lay a narrow chamber, smaller than Evelyn expected, lit only by a single oil lamp. A wooden chest sat on a raised platform, its surface scarred but intact.

Her pulse quickened. Every instinct screamed that the cipher had brought them to the right place.

The monk spoke again, this time slowly, his voice steady. Elias translated. "He says the chest belongs to those who understand what is inside, not those who seek to claim it."

Evelyn stepped forward, her breath shallow. The chest was sealed with a lattice of cord and a wax emblem that had long since cracked. She hesitated only a moment before breaking the brittle seal.

Inside lay a bundle of vellum scrolls wrapped in linen, edges frayed but ink still dark. The script was unlike anything she had seen. Ge'ez merged with Hebrew, layered with Greek inflections. The language was alive, as if its authors had written for readers centuries away.

Elias exhaled slowly. "This is it."

But before Evelyn could lift the first scroll, a faint sound reached them through the stone corridor. Not wind. Not bells. Boots.

Elias extinguished the lamp with a quick breath. Darkness enveloped them.

"They've found us," he whispered.

Outside the chamber, the footsteps multiplied. The organization had closed the distance. Their silence was practiced, precise.

Evelyn's hand brushed the edge of the chest. The scrolls were cold to the touch. She could feel their weight, not just ink and parchment, but centuries of defiance.

"Take what we can carry," Elias murmured.

As they worked in the dark, the ancient stone seemed to breathe around them. Footsteps moved closer, slow and certain. This was no random search. They were being cornered.

Evelyn tightened the satchel around the codices. For a heartbeat she met Elias's eyes in the dark. No words passed between them. The decision had already been made.

They were no longer just historians. They were fugitives carrying a truth others had spent centuries trying to bury.

The sound of boots on stone tightened around them like a noose. Each footfall was deliberate, trained, close. Elias motioned to Evelyn, two fingers cutting through the dark. She pulled the satchel tight across her chest, feeling the weight of the scrolls press against her ribs. Their discovery no longer belonged to the monastery. It belonged to the world outside and to danger.

The narrow corridor offered no easy retreat. To their left, the scriptorium opened toward the sleeping cells. To their right, the passage twisted downward into a network of older tunnels. Elias glanced at the ceiling, at the way the rock curved. "Monasteries this old," he whispered, "always have more than one way out."

They moved without light, their palms sliding along the cool wall. Behind them, a door creaked open, followed by the low murmur of unfamiliar voices. Evelyn felt the sound, low and precise, more than she heard it.

A lantern flared somewhere down the corridor. Shadows splintered across the stone.

Elias guided her toward a narrow arch she might have missed in daylight, a recess cut low into the wall, no wider than a single shoulder. They slipped through just as the footsteps reached the chamber they had left behind. A single beam of light swept across the scriptorium floor.

The tunnel sloped downward sharply, the air growing damp and metallic. The sound of dripping water echoed in the dark, faint but steady. They moved quickly, crouching low where the stone ceiling narrowed. Evelyn's breathing was shallow, controlled. She could feel the ancient dust on her tongue.

A distant thud broke the quiet behind them. Their pursuers had found the open chest.

Elias pressed a hand lightly to her arm. "They'll move fast now."

The tunnel forked. One path rose toward faint light, a shaft cut into the mountainside; the other plunged deeper into the dark. Elias hesitated for only a second. He chose the darkness.

"They'll expect us to run for the cliff exit," he whispered.

The descent was treacherous. Rocks shifted beneath their boots. The tunnel narrowed into a seam in the mountain, then widened into what felt like a natural cavern. Here the air smelled of moss and water. Somewhere nearby, a river moved through the stone.

A sudden scrape echoed above them. A single beam of lantern light cut across the cavern ceiling. They had been followed.

Evelyn pressed her back against the wall, breath held. A voice, a calm, measured baritone, carried down the tunnel. She couldn't make out the words, but she knew that tone. It was the same tone used by men who never needed to raise their voice to be obeyed.

Elias's hand brushed hers. A silent signal: Move.

They slipped along the cavern wall, feet finding shallow steps carved into the rock centuries before. Evelyn's hand grazed a faded carving, a cross intertwined with older Egyptian symbols. She felt a strange shiver, as if the stone itself recognized the scrolls she carried.

Another shout behind them. Louder this time.

Elias reached a narrow fissure that opened onto the cliffside. A rush of cold air slapped their faces, carrying the smell of rain and stone. Below, the valley stretched wide and black beneath the fading night. A storm gathered on the horizon.

Evelyn crouched low, scanning the sheer drop. Far below, a narrow ledge traced the cliff face, a goat path barely wide enough for two feet. It was the only way.

"They'll see us if we take it," she said softly.

"They'll catch us if we don't."

They stepped out into the night just as the first lantern glow broke through the fissure behind them. Elias moved first, hugging the wall, his boots skimming loose gravel. Evelyn followed, the satchel pressed close. The drop yawned beneath her like an open throat.

The storm wind howled against the stone, whipping her hair into her face. Lightning flared in the distance, illuminating the jagged ridge for a heartbeat. She caught a glimpse of figures at the fissure, three of them, silhouetted in the light.

A single gunshot cracked through the wind, sharp and clean. Stone splintered inches from her head.

"Faster," Elias hissed.

They moved along the ledge, muscles burning, the wind trying to peel them from the mountain. Another shot. This one missed Elias by a breath. Evelyn tasted iron at the back of her throat.

The ledge curved sharply and vanished behind a thick curtain of brush growing from the cliff wall. Elias pushed through first, pulling Evelyn after him. On the other side lay a narrow crevice, a hidden stairway carved deep into the rock.

Their pursuers shouted above the wind, their voices closer than she wanted to believe.

They half-slid, half-ran down the worn steps. At the base, the stairway opened onto the riverbank. The water surged through a gorge, fast and dark. A small, weathered skiff was tied to a post, its hull worn smooth.

Elias didn't hesitate. He cut the rope with his knife.

The current seized the boat the moment they pushed off. Lantern light flared above the cliff, shouts echoing against the stone. Evelyn dropped low, clutching the satchel tight as the skiff was swallowed by the dark river. The mountain retreated behind them, its silhouette black against the bruised sky.

For the first time since Axum, the pursuit fell silent. Only the river spoke now.

Elias turned toward her, his voice low but steady. "They know what we took."

Evelyn stared down at the satchel, at the ancient knowledge that now bound them to something far larger than themselves. The storm rolled across the highlands, a single flash of lightning splitting the night.

"They'll never stop," she said.

Elias's jaw tightened. "Then neither will we."

The river carried them for hours, its current twisting through a maze of black water and canyon stone. Wind scraped along the gorge walls, and the world above was little more than shadow. Neither spoke. The silence between them was the kind that follows survival, taut and unfinished.

The skiff bumped against a cluster of reeds where the river widened into a shallow basin. Dawn pooled faintly along the horizon, soft gray light bleeding into the night. Elias guided the boat to shore and dragged it beneath an overhang of rock where it would disappear from casual sight. The world here smelled of wet earth and cold stone, the kind of air that clung to bone.

Evelyn stepped onto the bank, boots sinking slightly into the mud. Her legs trembled from the climb and the chase, but her grip on the satchel remained iron. She eased it open just enough to glimpse the edges of the fragile, ancient, still intact scrolls. A breath she hadn't realized she'd been holding escaped her in a slow exhale.

"They won't be far behind," Elias said, scanning the opposite ridge. "But we've bought time."

She nodded, brushing damp hair from her face. "Enough?"

"Maybe."

A light drizzle began to fall, whispering against the leaves. Evelyn crouched near the water, letting the cold seep into her hands. Her pulse was still uneven; her mind caught between the stillness of the river and the echo of gunfire. The scrolls had survived centuries, and now their survival hung on two exhausted fugitives in the Ethiopian highlands.

Elias knelt beside her, laying out a small oilcloth. From his pack, he produced a compass, a map creased to near collapse, and a single battered thermos. The steam rising from the cup of bitter coffee between them felt almost unreal against the gray morning.

"The cipher points further north," Evelyn said, her voice low. "It wasn't just leading us to the monastery. There's something else beyond this. Something they feared enough to guard."

Elias nodded. "A text like this doesn't vanish into one vault. It spreads. Cells. Custodians." He traced a line across the map with his finger. "We follow the highland trail past Adwa. Beyond that, old caravan routes. Hidden monasteries. Places that don't show up on anything official."

She caught the flicker of caution in his expression. "They'll be ahead of us by then."

"Probably. But they'll also be louder. We'll move where they can't."

The storm thickened into a steady curtain of rain. In the distance, thunder rumbled, a sound so low it seemed to rise from the ground itself. The gorge around them blurred into mist, as if the world were deliberately folding in to hide their next step.

Evelyn unwrapped a single scroll just enough to see the script inside. The ink was dark and deliberate, the lettering neither wholly Ge'ez nor Hebrew nor Greek, but something in between, as if language itself had been woven to conceal. It wasn't just text. It was strategy.

Elias leaned closer. "You're smiling."

She shook her head, a quiet, disbelieving laugh escaping her. "No. I'm terrified."

The river shifted behind them, a deep, slow sound. Somewhere upstream, a bird called once and fell silent.

Elias stood, slinging his pack over one shoulder. "We can't stay here."

Evelyn tightened the satchel strap and rose. The rain had soaked through her clothes, cold against her skin, but the fear that had stalked her through the monastery now felt sharper, clearer. Not panic. Purpose.

As they climbed the embankment and vanished into the fog of the highlands, Evelyn glanced back once at the dark curve of the river. Their pursuers would follow. They always did. But for the first time, the chase no longer belonged only to the hunters.

The secret they carried was older than empire, older than the forces sent to bury it. And it was awake now.

The highlands rose in fractured steps, their silhouettes dissolving into low cloud. Rain softened the edges of everything: the trail, the horizon, the distinction between the living and the ancient. Evelyn and Elias moved in silence, their boots sinking into the slick red earth, each footfall swallowed by fog. The storm had become their ally, masking their path, dissolving their scent in wind and wet stone.

By late afternoon they had put miles between themselves and the river. The landscape opened to a narrow plateau where a grove of twisted junipers stood like sentinels against the mist. Elias dropped his pack beneath a gnarled trunk and unfolded the map again, its creases growing softer with each passing day.

Evelyn crouched beside him, unwrapping one of the scrolls with careful hands. She spread it across a strip of oiled cloth, shielding it from the drizzle. The script shimmered faintly in the gray light, black ink etched into vellum that bore the faint scent of smoke and dust. It wasn't just writing. It was deliberate architecture, language as concealment.

She traced the lettering with her fingertips. "See here," she whispered, "this isn't standard Ge'ez structure. The syntax mirrors Hebrew poetic form, but the glyph spacing follows a Coptic monastic cipher. And this..." she tapped a faint spiral motif at the corner, "...that's an astronomical marker. Not just text. Coordinates."

Elias leaned closer, the wind tugging at his jacket. "How old?"

"Older than anything Rome sanctioned. This was written to travel without being understood. If someone didn't know the languages, they'd think it's devotional verse."

A long silence stretched between them. The fog curled low along the plateau, muffling everything but the rain. Elias scanned the horizon while Evelyn worked, whispering fragments of the text to herself as if coaxing it awake.

"The pattern repeats every seven stanzas," she murmured. "But every seventh line hides a number. Align the numbers with the spiral... and it points here." She tapped a rough circle on the map northeast of their position.

Elias followed her finger. "A monastery?"

"Or something older."

The spiral was not just a cipher. It was a map keyed to the night sky. The coordinates aligned with a cluster of constellations that would only rise after sunset. Evelyn recognized the pattern, a celestial calendar woven into language. Whoever had hidden this text had trusted the stars more than paper.

Elias folded the map with quiet precision. "We move after dark. If they're tracking, they'll expect us to follow the road."

"And we won't," Evelyn replied.

The rain eased to a mist as the sun began its slow descent behind the highland ridges. They rested in silence, the world holding its breath around them. Evelyn ran her thumb along the vellum, feeling the grooves where ink had dried a millennium earlier. The people who wrote this had lived knowing they'd never see its end. She felt the weight of that trust settle against her chest.

By nightfall, the sky had cleared just enough for the stars to emerge cold, sharp points scattered across the black. Elias used the compass to align their bearing, but it was Evelyn's eyes that guided them. She followed the spiral embedded in the text, tracking constellations the way a desert traveler reads dunes.

They left the trail and cut through scrub and rock, moving fast but low. The wind moved against the slope, carrying the scent of wet stone. Somewhere in the distance, the sharp echo of engines broke the stillness faint but real.

"They're behind us," Elias said.

Evelyn didn't look back. "Then we're still ahead."

Hours later, they crested a ridge and saw it: a shape half-swallowed by fog, perched against the cliffside like something time had almost erased. A ruin, not a monastery, its towers broken, its arches blackened, the skeletal remains of a place older than recorded memory.

"This wasn't on any map," Elias murmured.

"It was never meant to be," Evelyn answered.

She tightened her grip on the satchel. The spiral had brought them here, just as it had brought others long before. Somewhere inside those stones lay the next piece of a gospel the world had spent centuries trying to silence.

Behind them, far down the valley, a single light blinked through the mist.

The hunt was closing in again.

The ruin loomed out of the fog like a memory the world had tried to forget. Its walls were fractured but standing, blackened arches jutting out of the cliffside like the ribs of a colossal beast. The wind moved through its hollow windows, low and restless, carrying with it the faint smell of ash, iron, and something older, something buried.

Elias halted just beyond the threshold. His boots sank slightly into the wet earth. "This place shouldn't exist," he murmured.

Evelyn tilted her head back, tracing the crumbling arch with her eyes. "Which is exactly why it does."

They crossed the uneven ground slowly, their flashlights slicing through the mist. Moss crawled up the walls, roots split the floor stones, but traces of deliberate geometry remained, a line of carved symbols, fractured mosaics, faint astronomical etchings worn nearly smooth by centuries of wind. This was not just a ruin. It had been built with purpose.

"Coptic structure," Evelyn said softly, crouching to brush debris from a carved lintel. "But the foundation... it's older. Pre-Christian. Syncretic site."

Elias scanned the periphery with the precision of someone who no longer trusted silence. "And someone still knows it's here. Look." He pointed to faint impressions in the mud recent, narrow-soled boots.

Their pursuers were closer than either of them liked.

Inside the largest chamber, the ceiling had partially collapsed, creating a jagged skylight that framed the stars. Rain dripped steadily through the opening, pattering onto a stone floor etched with concentric circles. The design matched the spiral cipher embedded in the scrolls. Evelyn's breath caught. "This is it."

She knelt in the center of the circles and laid the scroll across the cold stone. The lettering shimmered faintly beneath the beam of her flashlight, aligning with the carved lines on the floor as if the text itself had been waiting to return here.

Elias moved to the doorway, keeping watch, the faintest hum of engines somewhere out in the valley.

Evelyn traced the spiral pattern with her fingertips. The outer rings corresponded to coordinates, the inner circle to celestial markers. But the very center held a single symbol, a hybrid of Coptic, Hebrew, and an older Egyptian hieratic form. A sigil for "gateway."

She felt a chill climb the back of her neck. "This isn't a map," she whispered. "It's an instruction."

She pressed lightly on the stone where the sigil was carved. Something shifted. The circles rotated with a muted groan, ancient stone grinding against itself. Dust rose from the floor in a slow spiral as the center panel lowered a fraction, revealing a hollow space beneath.

Elias turned sharply. "Evelyn."

"I see it."

They knelt together, clearing the debris until a small wooden coffer emerged from the dark cavity. It was unlike the chest they'd found in the monastery: smaller, older, and sealed with a lattice of iron bands etched in archaic script. The wood was warm beneath Evelyn's fingertips, as though it had been waiting in the earth's breath all this time.

She ran her thumb along the inscription. "This isn't storage. It's preservation. Whoever hid this built it to outlast everything."

A sound fractured the quiet: the crack of a distant branch. Then another.

Elias straightened, flashlight sweeping the darkness. "They're here."

Evelyn lifted the coffer carefully, the weight of it far greater than its size suggested. She could feel the hum of the stone beneath her feet, the faint vibration of something old stirring awake.

Elias extinguished his light. They moved deeper into the ruin, their footsteps careful, the fog swallowing them whole.

Outside, the valley was no longer silent. A single engine growled in the distance, steady and controlled. Whoever had been following them was not searching anymore. They were closing in.

Elias leaned close, his whisper a thread in the dark. "Whatever's in that box, they've been after it for a very long time."

Evelyn's grip tightened around the coffer. The carvings pressed into her palms like a brand.

"Then we make sure they don't get it," she said.

They slipped through a broken archway at the rear of the ruin, following a narrow passage choked with roots and rubble. The old builders had carved escape routes into their sanctuaries. History had taught them that truth rarely survives in the open.

Behind them, footsteps entered the main chamber.

The footsteps inside the ruin were measured, unhurried, as if the pursuers already knew there was nowhere else to run. Their lantern beams cut through the fog and fractured against the crumbling stone, throwing jagged shadows across the walls. Evelyn felt them before she saw them, the weight of trained men moving in concert.

Elias motioned for silence. They pressed against the rough interior wall of a narrow side corridor, its ceiling low enough that they had to crouch. The coffer lay against Evelyn's chest, heavy and warm through her damp clothes, as though the object itself held its own pulse.

A voice drifted through the ruin. Calm. Controlled. A language designed to make obedience sound inevitable.

Elias leaned closer. "It's him."

Evelyn didn't need the name. The voice belonged to the one who never raised his tone and never needed to. She had heard it once before in a half-lit street in Alexandria, when their research still belonged to the realm of ideas and not survival.

"We're not here to harm you," the voice called out, echoing through the chamber like something carefully rehearsed. "You have something that doesn't belong to you."

Elias's jaw tightened. His whisper was barely audible. "They're stalling. Flushing us out."

Evelyn steadied her breath. The coffer dug into her ribs. The stone beneath her boots was slick with rain and moss, the ruin breathing with a kind of ancient stillness around the edges of danger.

A lantern beam swept the main chamber, catching fragments of broken arches and the spiral carved into the floor. The voice came again, softer this time. "This ends one way. Hand it over, and no one has to bleed for old stories."

Elias shifted, his hand brushing the handle of the climbing pick at his belt. "They think we're desperate," he murmured.

"We are," Evelyn whispered back, "but not careless."

A second voice joined the first, this one closer. Boots crunched against loose gravel, a sound too deliberate to be accidental. Someone was approaching the narrow passageway.

Elias caught Evelyn's gaze in the dim light. No words. Just the old language of shared resolve.

The first figure appeared at the entrance of the corridor, a tall shape backlit by the lantern glow, shoulders squared, steps slow. He held no gun in sight, but the weight of the weapon at his side was clear. Behind him, two others moved like shadows.

Evelyn pressed against the wall, heart hammering in a rhythm that felt almost synchronized with the ruin's distant creak. She remembered something her mentor had once said about power: The people who whisper are more dangerous than those who shout.

The man's voice was closer now. "You've gone far enough. Whatever you think you've found belongs to us."

Elias took a single step forward into the narrow shaft of light. "Then you've already made your first mistake," he said evenly.

The man's expression didn't change. But his fingers twitched once near his sidearm.

Evelyn tightened her grip on the coffer and glanced at the broken staircase behind them, half-collapsed but still passable. It wasn't an escape. It was a gamble.

Elias caught the look. "On three," he mouthed.

Rain hammered the roof of the ruin, filling the silence. One. The air grew sharp and cold. Two. The man in the corridor tilted his head slightly, as if sensing what came next. Three.

Elias struck first, not with the pick but with the lantern hook at his belt, yanking down the crumbling arch beside the corridor. Stone exploded into the passageway with a thunderous crack. Dust and fragments filled the air.

Evelyn didn't wait. She bolted up the broken stairwell, boots skidding against wet stone, the coffer pressed tight to her chest. Shouts erupted behind her. A single shot tore through the ruin, the sound reverberating like a blade across steel.

Elias followed, fast and silent, as the lantern light behind them turned jagged and chaotic. They burst through the upper archway into the cold night air.

The storm had thickened, the fog rolling in heavy sheets across the cliffside. Their pursuers were quick, but the ruin's collapsed corridors had bought them seconds, and in their world, seconds mattered.

"They're coming," Elias said, breath low and controlled.

"Then let's not be here when they arrive."

They vanished into the fog, the coffer clutched like a heartbeat between them, as the ruin behind them filled with the sound of pursuit.

The fog rolled in thick as wool, swallowing the ruin behind them. The night had turned cold, the kind of damp cold that clings to skin and finds its way into bone. The wind carried the scent of rain and iron. Evelyn's breath came in shallow bursts as they picked their way across the cliffside trail, the coffer a solid weight against her chest. Every few steps, loose gravel slid under their boots and disappeared soundlessly into the black void below.

Elias moved a few paces ahead, his silhouette a darker shape against the fog. He glanced back once, two fingers raised a signal. Slow. Listen.

Behind them, muted but unmistakable, came the sound of pursuit: boots scuffing stone, voices clipped low, the careful rhythm of men trained to hunt in silence. The ruin's upper arches were out of sight now, but the threat pressed in all the same, moving closer with the certainty of a tide.

"They're tracking us," Evelyn whispered.

"They're disciplined," Elias answered. "That's useful."

She frowned. "Useful?"

"If they're disciplined," he said quietly, "they're predictable."

The trail narrowed, hugging the cliff face so tightly that at times they had to turn their bodies sideways to pass. To their left, the fog swallowed everything; to their right, the stone wall was slick with rain, cold against their palms. The sound of the pursuers grew clearer, echoing in rhythmic intervals. Elias counted silently. Four men. No more.

Halfway along the trail, a jagged outcrop jutted over a sharp drop. Elias slowed, scanning the shape of the terrain as if reading a map etched in shadow. A natural choke point.

He turned to her. "We use it here."

She hesitated. "Elias"

He shook his head. "We're not going to win a chase. We're going to redirect it."

They pressed into a shallow cleft in the rock, the kind of gap easily overlooked in fog. Elias crouched low, pulling a line from his pack, a length of climbing rope frayed from hard use. Evelyn crouched beside him, pressing the coffer tight against her ribs. Her pulse drummed in her ears.

Voices emerged from the mist now, clearer, closer. One of the pursuers gave a low, clipped signal. Another answered. Their formation was tight; Elias could hear it in the cadence.

He threaded the rope through the slick rock face, creating a taut line that cut across the narrowest part of the path. One step too fast, and anyone coming through would find their balance stolen.

Evelyn's hand found his sleeve. Now.

The first lantern beam licked through the fog like a blade. A shadow moved through it, the lead man, silent and sure-footed. He never saw the rope. His boot caught, momentum carried him forward, and the sound that followed was soft and final: fabric scraping stone, a strangled grunt, then silence as the fog reclaimed him.

The others reacted fast. A burst of shouts. One gunshot cracked against the cliff wall, showering them with shards of rock. Evelyn flinched, covering the coffer with her body.

Elias pulled her back deeper into the cleft as the second man advanced cautiously, firing into the fog. The muzzle flash painted the mist in short, violent bursts of orange.

"Fall back," a voice hissed, calm, controlled. The leader. He hadn't fallen.

Elias leaned close to Evelyn. "He'll flank us. He's too experienced to push through."

"Then we don't give him the chance," she whispered.

Elias scanned the cliffside, then pointed toward a faint fissure barely visible through the fog, a narrow ledge cut into the rock, almost vertical. It led upward toward the ridge line. Dangerous, but defensible.

They moved in silence, climbing hand over hand, boots finding precarious holds. The fog thickened around them, dulling every sound except their own breath and the soft drag of rope against stone.

Below, the remaining pursuers fanned out, their movements slower now, more careful. They were hunting in fog they no longer controlled.

Evelyn reached the ridge first, pulling herself over the lip onto a stretch of windswept stone. The coffer thudded softly against the ground. Elias joined her seconds later, crouched low, scanning the gray abyss below. The fog swallowed everything but the faint bobbing of lantern light, drifting like specters far beneath.

For the first time that night, Evelyn exhaled fully.

Elias crouched beside her; voice barely audible against the wind. "They'll regroup. They won't retreat."

"No," she said quietly, tightening the satchel strap. "But neither will we."

Below them, the lanterns began to move again, methodical and relentless. But up here, on the ridge, they had vanished from their enemy's line of sight. The coffer sat between them like a sleeping heart, its carved sigils slick with rain, its presence undeniable.

Whatever lay inside had already drawn blood. And the hunt was far from over.

The ridge was a knife edge of stone, cold and slick beneath their boots. Wind coiled through the fog, low and constant, wrapping them in a cocoon of gray. The sound of pursuit had faded below, but neither of them trusted the silence. It was the kind that waited rather than ended.

Elias found a hollow in the rock just large enough to offer shelter. They settled into it like fugitives seeking not warmth, but invisibility. The storm had softened to a steady drizzle, whispering against the stone, erasing their footprints as if the night itself had chosen a side.

Evelyn set the coffer between them on a flat slab of rock. Even in the dim light of the small camping lamp Elias cupped in his hands, the sigils carved into the wood seemed to breathe. They were etched too deep and too clean to have weathered into this shape. It felt as if the box had been waiting for human hands to return.

Neither spoke at first. The air around them was too heavy for chatter.

Finally, Elias broke the quiet. "If they've chased this thing for centuries, it's not just a relic."

Evelyn nodded slowly. "No. It's a key."

She leaned closer, tracing the carved banding. Coptic. Hebrew. And an older Egyptian script so faint it barely revealed itself beneath the wet surface. Each language told only part of the story. Together, they formed a cipher, a seal meant to keep out those who didn't understand how to listen.

Elias kept watch, his eyes sweeping the ridge, the fog, the dark beyond. She worked methodically, whispering fragments of the text under her breath. A soft click answered her touch. One of the iron bands loosened with the sound of old metal releasing a breath it had been holding for centuries.

Another whisper. Another click.

The coffer opened with the weight of something both sacred and dangerous.

Inside, beneath layers of linen brittle as parchment, lay a single codex bound in faded leather. Its surface bore a faint impression of the same spiral sigil they had followed through Axum and the ruin. But what arrested Evelyn was the script along the spine: a seamless weaving of languages, Hebrew flowing into Coptic, Greek inflections threaded like ligatures, and geometric symbols that belonged to something far older than Christianity itself.

Elias leaned over, his voice low. "It's older than what we found in the monastery."

Evelyn carefully lifted the codex, its leather warm from the touch of the earth. The moment she opened it, the wind shifted, pressing against the hollow like a held breath. The first page was illuminated with a constellation map, star positions rendered in ink the color of rust. But these stars were not marked in the familiar Greco-Roman names. Their labels belonged to an earlier tongue.

"This isn't scripture," she whispered. "It's a map layered in theology."

As she turned the pages, patterns emerged: astronomical alignments paired with short liturgical passages, some phrased as prayers, others as directions. The stars served as keys to decode the text. The gospel wasn't meant to be read in linear time. It was meant to be unlocked in cycles like a celestial calendar.

Elias pointed to a cluster near the top of the map. "That alignment... it's real. I saw it on the chart last month. It's coming again."

Her pulse quickened. "Then the text isn't just history. It's timed."

The realization settled between them like an iron weight. This was no static relic. Someone, long ago, had written it for a moment still to come.

Elias poured a small arc of light across the next page. Lines of verse curved into star diagrams. The language flowed with intentional complexity, built to repel the unprepared. Evelyn's mind worked through the cipher instinctively, centuries folding beneath her fingertips. She found the first embedded phrase six words hidden in three languages and read it aloud softly.

The voice of the river leads to the house of light.

The wind seemed to catch on those words, curling against the rock like something listening. Elias met her gaze. "That's a location."

"Yes," she breathed. "And a warning."

Below, far down the ridge, a single lantern light bobbed once in the fog. Then another.

Their hunters were moving again.

Evelyn carefully closed the codex and wrapped it in the linen, the weight of it far greater than its size. She understood it now: this wasn't the end of their search but the beginning of something older and more precise, something written to outlast kingdoms.

Elias checked the edge of the ridge, then crouched beside her. "We'll need to move before dawn. They'll follow the high trail."

Evelyn's hand rested on the codex. The stars on the first page burned in her memory like embers. "Then we go where they can't."

The fog thickened once more, the wind whispering through the stones. Above them, the night sky opened just enough to reveal a sliver of constellations, the same pattern inked on the page.

The map wasn't pointing backward. It was pointing forward.

They left the ridge under a sky stretched thin with fading stars. The fog that had cloaked them through the night was breaking apart in pale ribbons, rising off the highlands like smoke from some invisible fire. Their breaths clouded in the chill air. Every step away from the ridge felt deliberate, the weight of the codex pressing against Evelyn's chest like a pulse she could almost hear.

Elias moved with the precision of a man who trusted terrain more than luck. His boots found narrow footholds between slabs of wet rock, guiding them down the back slope where no clear trail existed. The wind swept in from the east, carrying the damp scent of cedar and cold soil. Behind them, the ruin and the ridge had vanished into mist.

"They'll regroup at the cliff," Elias said quietly, eyes fixed on the slope below.

Evelyn adjusted the satchel strap. "They'll follow the spiral."

"They don't understand it like you do," he answered, but she heard the unspoken part: They will soon enough.

By midday the landscape changed, the high crags softening into rolling hills veined with ancient terraces. Shepherds once lived here. The land still remembered. Old walls leaned half-buried beneath wild grass, stones fitted with a precision that outlived the hands that built them. A narrow stream wound through the valley, its water, black with the reflection of low clouds.

Evelyn crouched at the bank and opened the codex again, shielding the pages from the wind with her body. The first map, the star alignment which had been easy to match. But here, in the margin, a secondary inscription had revealed itself overnight as the parchment absorbed the damp: a faint spiral of ink, etched in ghostly brown.

She traced it carefully. "This line follows the river's path. It's not just poetic language. It's literal. The house of light isn't on the ridge. It's buried along the water."

Elias crouched beside her, studying the curve of the valley. "This river moves north toward Lalibela. The old monastic networks passed through here."

"It predates Lalibela," she murmured. "Look at the carving." She tilted the page to catch the light. Along the edge of the spiral was an old Egyptian determinative, the symbol for hidden temple.

The wind picked up again, carrying the sound of distant movement down the valley. Evelyn closed the codex. "We're not alone."

They followed the river's bend, moving quickly but quietly, weaving through the terraces where fig trees clung to the stone. The world here felt old in a way that was not ruin but memory, a living presence pressed beneath the soil. As they walked, the water's voice grew louder, a steady rush that echoed against the valley walls.

By the time the sun had begun its slow descent, they reached a stretch of river that narrowed sharply, vanishing into a cleft between two jagged outcrops. The rock faces leaned toward one another like two great hands pressed together in prayer. A faint carving marked the entrance: the same spiral sigil.

Elias knelt, fingers brushing the stone. "This isn't a natural fissure."

"No," Evelyn said. "It's a threshold."

She ran her hand along the spiral. It wasn't painted. It had been chiseled cleanly, deliberately. The lines converged at a single point at the base of the rock. When she pressed her thumb there, the faintest vibration passed through the stone, as though the mountain itself recognized the gesture.

Behind them, the distant echo of boots reached their ears. Not close yet. But coming.

Elias stepped into the fissure first. The air inside was cooler, stiller, and dry. The light dimmed quickly, swallowed by a corridor carved deep into the mountain. Narrow niches lined the walls, empty now but still shaped for scrolls, reliquaries, or offerings. Their footsteps sounded impossibly loud in the enclosed space.

Evelyn carried the codex like a torch without flame. The spiral in its margins matched the spiral on the wall. This was where the cipher had always been leading.

As they moved deeper, the tunnel opened into a vast underground chamber. High above, a narrow shaft cut through the rock to the sky, letting in a single thread of dying sunlight. It spilled down like a column of gold, striking a raised platform at the center of the chamber.

Evelyn's throat tightened. "The house of light."

The platform was ringed with inscriptions, carved in a mixture of Hebrew and Coptic. But at the center stood something unexpected: a large circular mirror of polished obsidian, unblemished despite the centuries. Its surface caught the light from above and threw it across the chamber in fractured patterns that danced on the walls.

Elias circled it slowly, his boots silent on the stone. "This isn't just a temple."

Evelyn lowered her voice to a whisper. "It's a signal."

The codex matched the chamber with unnerving precision. Every inscription, every angle of light had been planned. This wasn't a place of worship. It was a place of activation.

Far above them, the sound of the wind shifted. Then faint, distant, but clear, a metallic click.

Elias's eyes hardened. "They've found the fissure."

Evelyn held the codex close. She understood now: the text wasn't just a record of the past. It was an instruction for the future, a future now colliding with the present in the dark of this chamber.

"They're coming," Elias said.

She nodded slowly; her eyes fixed on the obsidian mirror. "Then they're too late."

The chamber swallowed sound. Even the wind outside seemed to hold its breath. The single shaft of fading sunlight burned a golden circle into the platform, catching the black surface of the obsidian mirror. Its reflected light scattered across the walls in fractured, trembling arcs.

Evelyn stood near the platform; the codex pressed against her ribs. She could hear the echo of boots moving through the fissure, careful, deliberate, and close. Elias moved to the shadows near the entrance, lowering himself behind a column of stone. His hand hovered near the climbing pick, his breathing steady.

The voices arrived first. Controlled. Calm. A rhythm they had come to recognize. The leader's tone carried the same quiet authority that had haunted the ruin days before.

"You've done well," the voice called out, its calmness more threatening than a gunshot. "No one's come this far in centuries. But it ends here."

Evelyn's fingers tightened on the codex. The way he said centuries told her what she had suspected: these men weren't scavengers or academics. They were custodians of suppression, heirs to a long, careful erasure.

The first beam of a flashlight slashed through the darkness, catching on the black mirror and splitting into a dozen thin shards of light. Three figures stepped into the chamber, their movements precise, their eyes scanning in unison. Elias counted their footsteps without looking. Three.

The leader stopped just inside the circle of light, his face still half in shadow. He didn't raise his weapon. He didn't need to. "You're holding something that doesn't belong to you."

Evelyn's voice was low but steady. "If it never belonged to anyone, how can you claim it?"

That earned her a thin, humorless smile. "Because history belongs to the ones who keep it buried."

Elias shifted slightly in the shadows, silent.

The leader lifted his hand, not to strike, but to gesture toward the platform. "Do you even understand what you've brought here?"

Evelyn did. Not fully. Not yet. But enough. The codex had been pointing to this chamber all along. The obsidian mirror wasn't a relic; it was an anchor. It reflected not just light but alignment. Above them, stars were shifting into position. She could almost feel it, like a pressure in the air, an invisible thread being pulled taut.

She took a step toward the platform. "I understand enough."

One of the men raised his weapon slightly. Elias tensed but didn't move. The leader lowered the man's arm with a single glance. "No," he said softly. "Let her."

Evelyn laid the codex on the platform. The fading sunlight caught the spiral etched into its cover, igniting it in a muted gleam. She opened the first page and placed her palm on the star map.

The leader took a step forward, his voice dropping to a whisper. "Be careful. That mirror doesn't illuminate. It reveals."

The light through the shaft above narrowed to a blade as the sun slid lower in the sky. When it struck the mirror's exact center, the black glass flared, not bright, but deep, as if the darkness itself had awakened. The light scattered across the chamber in sharp, geometric shapes, aligning perfectly with the engravings on the walls.

Elias whispered, "She's triggering it."

The leader's voice carried over the wind and stone. "And she doesn't know what happens next."

Evelyn didn't flinch. "Neither do you."

The light sharpened further. A low, resonant hum rolled through the chamber, not mechanical, but organic, like the vibration of something buried far below. The men stiffened, guns shifting slightly as their leader's composure flickered. For the first time, Evelyn saw uncertainty in his face.

Elias stepped from the shadows, climbing pick in hand. "Looks like you don't control everything after all."

The leader's eyes narrowed. "Control isn't the point. Containment is."

The hum deepened, vibrating through the floor. The sigils on the walls ignited faintly, one by one, like embers remembering fire. Evelyn could feel the codex's leather warming beneath her palm. She realized this was no ritual meant to summon anything. It was a record unlocking itself for whoever could bring the right alignment, a language designed to outlive conquerors.

The leader lifted his weapon now, slowly, deliberately. "Step away."

Elias moved forward, placing himself between Evelyn and the gun. "You'll have to shoot through me."

The leader's eyes didn't flicker. "If I have to."

Another vibration rolled through the chamber, shaking loose a shower of dust from the ceiling. The mirror's reflection wasn't scattering now. It was focusing narrowing into a single point of light that speared across the room, cutting through fog and shadow, and struck a small recess in the far wall. A lock. A door.

Evelyn's heart pounded. "It's opening."

The leader barked something in a language she didn't recognize. His men spread out, their training flawless. They weren't here to study or to witness. They were here to take.

Elias's voice was calm, almost too calm. "We need to move."

Evelyn closed the codex with one hand, her fingers burning from the heat radiating off the mirror. The sound of the stone door grinding open filled the chamber. Beyond it lay only darkness but not the empty kind. A darkness that waited.

The leader turned his gun on Evelyn. "You take one step into that room, and history dies with you."

She met his eyes. "No. It dies when no one dares to step through."

Then she moved.

The sound of stone grinding against stone filled the chamber like the breath of something long asleep. The door's opening was slow, deliberate, as though time itself needed permission to let anyone in. Cold air rushed from the darkness beyond, carrying the scent of earth that had not been disturbed in centuries.

Evelyn didn't wait for the leader's next warning. She slipped past the platform and into the threshold, the codex clutched tight in one hand. The darkness swallowed her almost instantly, the world behind shrinking to a sliver of fractured light.

"Evelyn!" Elias's voice echoed, low and tense.

Boots pounded against stone. The leader's men reacted as trained soldiers do, one covering the entrance, the others moving to flank. But they didn't fire. Not yet. They wanted the codex intact.

Elias moved after her, his shoulder grazing the narrowing door. He felt the hum through the stone, a low vibration in the marrow of the walls. Whatever mechanism had been set in motion, it would not remain open forever.

The corridor beyond the door was narrow and cut with uncanny precision. The walls were smooth, lined with faint etchings that caught the dim glow of their flashlights. Evelyn kept moving, guided by the spiral patterns that now made sense in a way they hadn't before. The codex wasn't just a map. It was the key to reading the architecture itself.

Behind them, the pursuers entered. Their boots no longer echoed like intruders; they sounded like predators.

"Faster," Elias murmured.

The corridor opened suddenly into a vast underground chamber, larger than the mirror room above. It was circular, domed, its ceiling carved with constellations. At the center stood a tall obelisk of smooth basalt, polished to a mirror sheen. The floor around it was inlaid with star diagrams, identical to the first page of the codex.

Evelyn stopped in her tracks. The alignment wasn't symbolic. It was active. A single shaft of light from the mirror room above reached through a carved slit in the ceiling, striking the top of the obelisk like a thread of gold. The entire chamber was breathing, a soft pulse of light and shadow.

Elias reached her side, breathing hard. "This place... it's alive."

"It's recording," she whispered. "It's been waiting."

The leader's voice carried through the corridor. Calm. Always calm. "Hand it over, Dr. Reed."

His silhouette emerged from the darkness, followed by two armed men. They spread out along the curve of the wall, careful, professional. They didn't rush. Predators never rush when their prey is cornered.

Evelyn backed toward the obelisk. The codex pulsed faintly against her palm, warmth bleeding through the leather. She looked up at the carvings, star maps, lines of Coptic script, Hebrew phrases, fragments of Egyptian solar hymns. This wasn't a single culture. It was a fusion. An intentional weaving of truths meant to survive whoever ruled above ground.

"You don't even know what this is," she said.

The leader stepped into the light, his face finally clear. He was older than she expected. Sharp eyes. No cruelty. Just conviction. "I know enough. I know what happens if it's released."

Elias moved slightly to her left, angling himself between her and the gun barrel. "If it's so dangerous," he said evenly, "why have you spent your life making sure no one finds it?"

"Because some stories are more dangerous when told than when buried."

Evelyn shook her head. "Or maybe they're dangerous to the ones who buried them."

For the first time, something flickered across the man's face, not doubt, but memory. He gave a small nod, almost respectful. "You think the truth will save anyone. It won't. It will unmake everything they've built to keep the world from tearing itself apart."

She took a single step backward until the obelisk was at her spine. Her fingers brushed a shallow groove in the stone. It felt like an inscription worn smooth by centuries of hands. The codex seemed to hum against it, as if recognizing a twin.

Elias lowered his voice. "Evelyn."

She understood. They had only one chance. The door above would not remain open forever, and their pursuers would not leave without the codex.

The leader raised his gun. "Put it on the floor."

Evelyn held his gaze. "No."

The chamber trembled faintly, a resonance climbing through the floor like a living thing. She pressed the codex into the groove. A soft, almost inaudible sound followed, not mechanical, not stone, but something deeper. The obelisk responded. Light rippled down its length like water, spilling across the diagrams on the floor.

One of the soldiers shouted, stumbling backward as the inlaid stars flared to life.

The leader's calm cracked for the first time. "What did you do?"

Evelyn's voice was steady now. "I opened it."

The chamber roared with the sound of stone shifting, an ancient heartbeat surging awake. The star lines converged beneath their feet, casting a harsh light up the walls. Shadows dissolved into brilliance.

Elias grabbed her arm, pulling her to the edge of the platform. The soldiers moved too late. One tried to fire, but the floor itself cracked between them, not with destruction, but with design. It was as if the chamber had chosen its side.

The leader stood his ground; eyes locked on Evelyn. "You have no idea what you've unleashed."

She met his stare, the weight of centuries behind her. "Neither do you."

And the floor opened beneath them.

The floor did not collapse so much as yield.

For a heartbeat, Evelyn felt weightless, suspended in a column of light and dust as the star inlays split open along precise geometric seams. Then the stone fell away beneath them like petals folding inward. The world narrowed to motion and echo, boots scraping against slick walls, the hiss of air rushing through ancient channels, the dull thunder of their pursuers above shouting into chaos.

Elias caught her arm mid-fall. Together they slammed into a sloping passage, stone worn smooth by centuries of flowing water. Momentum carried them down, tumbling through darkness lit only by the fading glow from the chamber above. They hit solid ground hard, the impact reverberating up their bones.

For several breaths, the only sound was their ragged breathing and the slow, patient drip of underground water.

Evelyn blinked into the dark. A thin band of light spilled down from the fractured ceiling above, catching the swirling dust like ash in a shaft of fire. Her hands clenched around the codex. It was warm and alive in a way parchment should not be.

Elias pushed himself upright, his voice low and steady despite the fall. "We're still inside."

Evelyn followed his gaze. The lower chamber stretched outward in a perfect circle, larger than the mirror hall, older than the obelisk room above. Its walls were carved with reliefs so intricate they seemed to breathe, figures with both human and animal features, stars bound to their wrists like chains, scrolls carried in hands that had never existed.

The ceiling was high, domed, a single spiral carved from its center outward. It looked less like architecture and more like intention made stone.

"This isn't a vault," Evelyn whispered. "It's a memory."

At the center of the floor stood a pedestal carved from black basalt. Upon it rested a sphere of polished alabaster veined with faint gold, half-buried in dust but untouched by time. Thin rays of light from the upper chamber's fractures fell across it like reverent fingers.

Elias approached slowly, scanning the edges of the room. "Someone built this to last forever."

"Or to wait," Evelyn murmured.

The codex trembled faintly in her hands, a subtle vibration that felt less like weight and more like recognition. She stepped closer to the sphere. The same spiral sigil was carved into its surface, matched exactly to the cipher embedded in the codex's first page.

Elias exhaled softly. "This is what they were guarding."

She nodded. "Not a manuscript. A conduit."

The sphere wasn't an object meant to be displayed. It was a mechanism, a keyhole that required a story, not a key. Evelyn knelt, laying the codex on the pedestal's edge. When she opened it, the inscriptions caught the meager light and pulsed once, as if syncing with the chamber's carved lines.

The air shifted. The soft drip of water stopped, replaced by a low resonance threading through the walls. Dust shivered on the stone floor.

Elias stepped back, voice low. "Evelyn..."

She heard it too: a whispering sound, faint at first, like distant voices trapped between walls. It wasn't language as much as cadence, an old rhythm carried down through time. She touched the sphere with her fingertips, and the sound grew louder, layered, harmonic, like a hundred prayers overlapping.

"It's a recording," she said softly. "But not on paper. On stone. On light."

As she pressed the codex against the spiral, a beam of golden light arced upward from the sphere, striking the spiral carved into the dome. The reliefs along the walls illuminated one by one, casting the chamber into a living constellation.

Images flickered across the curved surface: ships under desert stars, scribes at stone tables, Coptic monks carrying fragments of a text across sand and sea, each generation passing it into the hands of the next. It wasn't a single story; it was a lineage.

Elias stood motionless. "They built this so the truth couldn't be erased."

Evelyn's eyes burned with the weight of it. "So, it could wait."

Above, faint shouts echoed down through the fissure. The leader and his men were coming.

She turned to Elias, her voice barely a whisper. "If they get down here, they'll bury it again. They'll bury everything."

He nodded once. The time for running was gone. What they carried now was no longer just a discovery. It was a choice.

Evelyn's hand hovered over the glowing sphere. She could feel its heat against her skin, not like fire but like something living, pulsing in rhythm with the codex and the carvings on the wall.

Elias crouched beside her, his voice low, steady. "Whatever you're about to do... do it fast."

A metallic clatter above, boots on stone, ropes unfurling into the dark. The chamber was no longer theirs alone.

Evelyn looked up at the glowing spiral overhead. "Then we show them what they tried to bury."

She pressed her palm to the sphere.

The light roared to life.

The chamber did not simply brighten, it awakened.

The golden light surged outward from the alabaster sphere like a living tide, racing along the carved spirals in the floor, climbing the walls, and threading itself through the reliefs. Dust lifted from the stone as if gravity itself had loosened its grip. Evelyn felt it vibrate beneath her palm, not just heat but memory, the weight of centuries pressing into her bones.

The ceiling dome flared with a radiant constellation. Each star carved into the stone blazed with light, spinning slowly into alignment. The walls no longer felt inert. They breathed. They remembered.

Elias staggered back a step, eyes wide. "Evelyn... it's reading itself."

"No," she whispered. "It's telling itself."

The reliefs began to move. Not like film. Like presence. Figures of ancient scribes emerged from the stone in faint translucent layers, not flesh but echoes. They walked across the walls as though on a stage long forgotten. Scribes dipped their pens. Desert ascetics carried parchment and clay tablets through the sands. Monks wrapped scrolls in linen and hid them inside earthen jars. Centuries collapsed into seconds.

And then a voice. Not human in the ordinary sense. It rose through the chamber like a wind carrying every language at once. Aramaic. Coptic. Greek. Hebrew. Words braided together, not translated but harmonized.

"The word was not given to be owned. It was sown to be found."

Evelyn's knees nearly buckled. The codex pulsed in her hands, alive in perfect resonance with the voice. This wasn't the text being read. This was the text.

Elias turned sharply toward the entrance. Ropes dropped from the fissure above. Black silhouettes slid down, flashlights slicing through the luminous air. The leader landed first, gun drawn but eyes narrowing as the sight struck him. His men followed, fanning out with practiced precision but none could fully ignore the way the chamber itself seemed to push against their presence, as if it knew them.

The voice swelled, filling the space like an ocean:

"When those who heard the word fall silent, the stone will speak."

The soldiers froze for a heartbeat. The leader didn't. He stepped forward, the weapon steady but his gaze flickering between Evelyn, the sphere, and the living script spilling across the walls. He had known something lay below, but not this.

"Shut it down," he said.

Evelyn didn't move. "I can't."

"You will."

The chamber responded before she could. The spiral in the dome reached its full alignment, locking into place like the turning of a celestial mechanism. A surge of light erupted upward not blinding but absolute. For an instant, their shadows disappeared.

The men raised their guns, but the light bent around them like a shield, refracting their beams, swallowing their aim. The leader barked an order; the sound fell flat, muted by the living hum of the chamber.

Elias edged closer to Evelyn, his voice barely audible. "It's... protecting itself."

The leader advanced anyway, each step more forced than the last. His weapon trembled in his grip, not from fear but from the pressure in the air, a weight that turned each movement into defiance.

"You don't understand what you're waking," he hissed. "This isn't a treasure. It's a fracture. It breaks worlds."

Evelyn looked up at him; calm now in a way she hadn't expected. "Then why bury it?"

"Because once it's spoken," he said, almost gently, "you can't unhear it."

Behind him, the echoes of the past continued to play out. Hands passed scrolls from age to age. Voices rose in unison. Not a single author, but a chorus.

The leader leveled his gun at the sphere. Evelyn stepped in front of it. The barrel didn't waver.

"Move."

She didn't.

Elias moved to her side. The chamber's hum deepened low, resonant, deliberate. It was no longer background sound. It was watching.

"You'll destroy nothing," Evelyn said. "Because this isn't yours to silence."

The light surged again, sharper this time. It struck the gun like a hammer. Metal hissed in the leader's hand, and the weapon shattered against the floor, its pieces skittering across the glowing stone.

His men fired reflexively. The bullets disintegrated in the air like ash meeting a furnace.

The leader took a single step back. For the first time since she had met him, Evelyn saw something behind his control. Not fear but recognition.

"This is why we buried it," he whispered.

Evelyn's voice was steady. "And this is why it survived."

The chamber's light condensed, spiraling upward into a column that pierced the dome. Ancient voices rose into a single, clear note that hung in the air like the toll of a bell. The reliefs on the walls shifted one final time, revealing a map. Not a map of land. Of lineage. Lines of transmission. Alexandria. Sinai. Axum. Across oceans. Through time.

Elias stepped closer to the wall, tracing the glowing threads with his eyes. "They left a record of where it went."

"Not just a record," Evelyn breathed. "A path."

Above them, the fissure glowed faintly as if the night itself had bent down to listen. The leader stood motionless now, caught in the same truth he had spent a lifetime trying to suppress. His men lowered their useless weapons.

For the first time, the chamber was utterly silent, not because the story had ended, but because it had entered the world again.

Evelyn turned toward Elias. "They can't bury it now."

He nodded once. "Then we run not to hide it. To finish it."

The leader said nothing. But in his eyes, Evelyn saw something dangerous: not defeat, but a decision.

The silence after the revelation was thin, stretched tight like glass. Evelyn felt it in her chest, not stillness, but the breath before something breaks.

The column of light above the sphere began to shimmer, the edges bending inward. The resonance in the walls shifted from low and steady to sharp, urgent. Dust shook loose from the carvings. Somewhere deep beneath their feet, an ancient mechanism stirred.

Elias caught it first. "It's closing."

Evelyn turned to the fissure they'd fallen through. The ropes above swayed, but the opening was already narrowing, a grinding rumble rolling through the chamber like a distant avalanche. Stone shifted with purpose, not collapse sealing itself.

The leader's men reacted fast. One barked an order. They fired grappling lines toward the fissure, pulling taut, but the hooks scraped against the tightening stone and slipped free. The leader watched the chamber with clenched fists, his mask of control slowly cracking around the edges.

"You've started something you don't understand," he said, voice low, almost reverent now.

Evelyn backed toward the pedestal, snatching up the codex. "Maybe. But I'm not the one who's been hiding it for centuries."

The sphere dimmed slightly but continued to pulse with an inner glow. Its light threaded into the fissure above, as if holding the last door open. The chamber itself seemed to decide who would leave, and who would stay buried.

Elias's eyes swept the edges of the room. "There," he said, pointing to a narrow passage half-hidden behind a relief of a veiled woman holding a scroll. The air moved faintly there, an old escape route, carved not for intruders but for custodians.

Evelyn nodded. "Go."

The soldiers noticed their movement a heartbeat too late. Elias ducked behind a pillar, disarming one man with a brutal strike to the wrist. His gun clattered uselessly across the glowing floor. Evelyn slid past the leader; the codex pressed against her chest like a heartbeat.

The leader didn't chase. He turned his gaze to the sphere, as though memorizing it. Or perhaps, mourning it.

Elias reached the opening first. The passage was narrow, carved with the same spiral motifs, but damp with centuries of trapped air. "It leads up," he said. "Probably back toward the surface."

"Then move," Evelyn whispered.

Behind them, the chamber's hum rose to a howl. Light from the sphere shot upward like a flare, striking the fissure with blinding force. Stone screamed as it shifted. One of the soldiers made a desperate leap for the ropes, but the opening slammed shut around him, cutting off the light. His scream was brief.

The leader turned toward them, framed in gold. For an instant, his eyes met Evelyn's no fury, no plea. Only inevitability.

"Run," he said quietly.

Then the chamber roared.

Evelyn and Elias pushed into the passage, the walls vibrating around them. The air grew heavier, the light behind flaring and fading in pulses. They climbed over broken steps and ducked beneath low arches, following the faint upward pull of fresher air.

The rumble behind them deepened. Dust fell from the ceiling. Stone ground against stone. Whatever had been asleep for centuries was locking itself away again.

Elias helped her over a collapsed lintel, his hand steady despite the tremors. "Keep moving," he muttered. "Don't look back."

But Evelyn did just once.

Through the narrowing passage, she saw the leader still standing near the sphere, its light wrapping around him like a halo. He wasn't running. He was staying. Guarding the silence one last time.

The tunnel twisted sharply upward. The air cooled. A faint wind brushed against her face, carrying the scent of dust and night. Then, a thin crack of moonlight appeared ahead.

Elias shoved at the last stone door, and it groaned open to reveal the ravine's upper edge, a jagged mouth hidden beneath a shelf of crumbling rock. They stumbled out into the night, lungs filling with clean, cold air. The stars above were sharp, indifferent.

The ground behind them rumbled like distant thunder. The earth sealed itself in a single, shuddering breath.

Evelyn collapsed to her knees, clutching the codex. The moonlight washed across its surface. It no longer felt like an artifact. It felt like a pulse.

Elias crouched beside her, listening to the fading tremor below. "It's gone."

She shook her head. "Not gone. Waiting again."

They sat there for a long moment, the desert wind whispering through the stones. The night felt heavier now, threaded with something vast and awake beneath their feet.

Elias glanced at her. "You realize what happens now?"

She looked down at the codex, its faint glow still warm against her palms. "Yes. They'll come after it again."

"Not just them."

She nodded. "Then we don't run from it. We run with it."

Far below, in the sealed chamber, the sphere pulsed once more, not a warning. A promise.

The night was a hollowed-out silence, broken only by the wind moving through the ravine. Evelyn sat with her back against a jagged boulder, the codex resting in her lap. Its weight was not physical. It was history itself, warm against her palms, as though still tethered to the chamber below.

Elias stood a few feet away, scanning the horizon. The desert stretched endless in every direction, a black ocean under starlight. But he wasn't looking for landmarks. He was listening. The absence of sound was louder than noise.

"They'll be moving," he said finally.

Evelyn didn't look up. "They were already moving."

"They'll come in force this time. The kind that doesn't ask questions."

The codex gave a faint, rhythmic glow with each breath she took, as if alive to the pulse of the night. She ran her thumb along its edge, tracing the raised embossing that mirrored the spiral they'd seen beneath the earth.

"This wasn't just a vault," she said softly. "It was a relay. It was meant to wake up."

Elias turned toward her, his face etched in the cold light. "Then we just rang a bell that's been silent for centuries."

She exhaled slowly. "And everyone who's been waiting to keep it silent heard it."

A soft crunch of gravel drew his attention. He crouched low, pulling her down with a steady hand. Headlights flickered far down the valley floor, faint, but real. Not the careless swing of wanderers. Convoy lights. Coordinated.

"They're fast," he murmured.

"They knew we'd surface somewhere." Evelyn closed the codex and fastened the leather strap, locking its glow back beneath the cover. "We need to move."

Elias nodded toward the west ridge. "There's a supply cache two clicks from here. Old survey station. If we make it, we can get comms out and disappear before they tighten the net."

"Disappear where?"

"Anywhere that isn't here."

But she heard the unspoken calculation in his voice. This wasn't a sprint. This was the beginning of a chase with no finish line.

They moved quickly and low, weaving between boulders and the broken teeth of the ravine. The headlights below grew brighter, cutting through the night with surgical precision. Whoever the leader had called in, they were professionals. Not archaeologists. Not scholars. Operators.

The ground sloped upward, the rocks sharp and cold beneath their palms as they climbed. The desert air thinned with altitude, biting at their lungs. Evelyn forced herself to focus on the rhythm of her breathing and the weight of the codex against her side.

Halfway up, Elias stopped and glanced back. A column of figures had entered the ravine floor, their movements disciplined and fast. One of them paused at the mouth of the fissure. He didn't need to go in. He knew what had happened below.

"Whoever was left down there bought us maybe ten minutes," Elias said.

Evelyn didn't answer. She could still see the leader standing near the sphere, haloed in gold. His silence had not been defeat. It had been a choice. A delay.

They reached the top of the ridge and dropped low behind a cluster of wind-carved stones. The desert stretched endlessly beyond. Distant hills lay like sleeping giants beneath the stars. A faint blue shimmer on the horizon marked the direction of the old survey station.

"Do we even know what's in this?" Elias asked, keeping his voice low.

Evelyn's fingers brushed the codex. "Enough to burn through history."

"Or rewrite it."

She met his gaze. "That's what they're afraid of."

Down below, a helicopter blade cut the stillness. A single searchlight swept across the canyon wall. The sound rolled up the ridge a second later, thick and heavy.

Elias's jaw tightened. "We're out of time."

They broke into a run, careful but fast, staying in the shadow of the rocks. The searchlight moved like a predator's gaze, slow, deliberate, patient. The convoy below split, some fanning toward the fissure, others branching to higher ground.

Evelyn stumbled once on loose shale, but Elias caught her before she fell. The codex pressed against her ribs like a living heart. Every step away from the ravine felt less like escape and more like escalation.

The desert wind carried the distant hum of rotor blades. The world behind them was waking up, not with wonder, but with the measured precision of an old machine.

Elias glanced at her as they moved. "They'll never stop now."

She looked straight ahead. "Then neither will we."

A pale line of light on the horizon marked the survey station, a forgotten ruin of rusted steel and broken glass. But to them, it was a thread, however thin, leading them out of the immediate reach of the hunters below.

The chamber had spoken. The codex was no longer a secret. And somewhere in the dark, power was shifting.

The survey station emerged from the darkness like the ribcage of a long-dead animal. Corrugated steel panels rusted into a dull ochre clung to the rocky slope, half buried by years of sandstorms. The wind moaned through broken antennae, carrying with it the dry breath of the desert night.

Elias approached first, checking for signs of tampering. The door hung crooked on its hinges but gave under pressure, groaning softly as he pushed it open. The interior smelled of machine oil, dust, and old metal, the ghosts of utility left behind when the world forgot about this place.

Evelyn followed, her boots crunching on grit. Inside, the walls were lined with abandoned relay equipment and cracked monitors that hadn't seen power in decades. But in the center of the room stood a single functioning object: a portable satellite uplink, left behind by someone who had used this place far more recently.

Elias's jaw tightened. "Someone's been here."

"Friend or enemy?" Evelyn asked.

He checked the uplink's status lights. A faint green glow pulsed steadily. "Either way, it works. That's what matters."

Evelyn set the codex down on a table covered in dust, its leather cover catching the dim lantern light like the surface of something alive. For a moment, neither of them spoke. The wind rattled the walls, a hollow, restless sound that seemed to echo the weight between them.

Elias knelt beside a cracked console, prying open a panel with practiced ease. "We can patch through to a secure channel. I know someone who still owes me a favor in Ankara. They can get us off grid, at least long enough to breathe."

Evelyn's gaze didn't leave the codex. "We're past favors, Elias."

"I know."

He didn't have to say what they were both thinking. The moment the chamber spoke, the story ceased belonging to them. Every intelligence agency, covert organization, religious order, and power structure that had kept it buried would now feel the tremor.

She brushed away a layer of dust from the table, revealing faded survey markings etched into the surface. A date was scratched in the corner: 1974. Another hand had carved something newer beneath it, a spiral. Her breath caught.

"They were here," she whispered.

Elias looked up. "The same people?"

She nodded. "Or the ones before them."

The spiral wasn't just a symbol. It was a marker, a thread in a long, hidden network of watchers, custodians, and silencers. The codex was never meant to vanish. It was meant to circulate in the dark, moving just far enough to stay alive and just hidden enough to stay forgotten.

The satellite uplink chirped softly. Elias was already entering a string of coordinates from memory. Evelyn crossed the room, watching the readout as the system came online. A narrowband signal, encrypted and weak, pulsed like a heartbeat.

"Who are you calling?" she asked.

"Someone who doesn't like governments any more than they like zealots."

The screen flickered, then steadied. A low hum filled the room as the transmission locked. No voice yet, just an open channel, waiting.

Evelyn leaned against the table, fingers drumming against the codex. "They'll trace the activation."

"Yeah," Elias said. "But not fast enough."

He turned to face her fully then, his voice low and steady. "We can't just run forever with that thing. You know that."

"I know."

"They'll hunt us, but they'll also hunt each other. You've seen what this does. They won't let it sit in anyone's hands."

Evelyn exhaled through her teeth. "Then we don't hold it. We move it. Force it into the light where no one can bury it again."

"Broadcast it?"

"Not just broadcast it. Unleash it."

Outside, the wind shifted. A distant hum grew louder mechanical, rhythmic, unmistakable. Not convoy engines this time. Rotor blades.

Elias grabbed his pack. "They're here."

Evelyn slid the codex into its protective satchel, the weight settling against her shoulder like a living pulse. The channel on the uplink crackled, and a voice finally came through distorted, clipped, but human.

"Reed. Mallick. We've been listening. And yes, we know what you've found."

Elias froze. "That was fast."

The voice continued, low and deliberate. "You're not the only ones who've been waiting for that chamber to open."

Evelyn's stomach tightened. "Who are you?"

A soft chuckle on the line. "The ones who've been listening to the stones while the rest of the world pretended, they were mute."

Elias glanced toward the door. The thrum of rotors was getting closer, sharper.

The voice spoke again, calm and final. "If you want to live, follow the spiral."

The transmission cut to static.

Outside, the first searchlight swept across the hillside.

Elias shouldered his pack. "I hate when they sound like they know everything."

Evelyn tightened the strap on the codex. "Good. Then we're exactly where we're supposed to be."

They slipped into the night as the first boots hit the ground around the station. The sky above was no longer empty.

The wind tore at their faces as they ran. The helicopter swept low over the desert, its searchlight cutting across the cracked earth like a blade. Evelyn and Elias moved fast along the shadow line of the ridge, using every scrap of darkness the night would give them. The codex thumped against Evelyn's side with each step, its warmth steady, its presence impossible to ignore.

Elias glanced back. The station was already swarmed by black silhouettes moving with the precision of trained operators. Whoever had landed wasn't a scavenger team. They were clean, coordinated, and silent.

"Down slope," he hissed. "We need cover."

They scrambled down a wash choked with dry brush and stone. The searchlight swept past overhead, then arced back, circling. The wind from the rotors pressed the desert flat around them. Evelyn crouched low behind a boulder, her heart hammering. Elias leaned against the stone beside her, scanning the horizon.

"They're triangulating."

"They already know where we are," she said.

"Yeah," he replied. "I just want to make it expensive for them to catch us."

A faint sound drifted on the wind, not boots, but engines. More vehicles moving in from the south, closing the perimeter. Evelyn tightened her grip on the strap of the codex. "We're boxed in."

"Not yet."

Elias pulled a small transceiver from his pack, keyed in a code, and held it to his ear. The channel was silent at first, then a burst of static, then a single tone, low and pulsing, like a heartbeat.

Evelyn frowned. "What is that?"

"Our extraction," Elias said. "If they're who I think they are."

"Who are they?"

Before he could answer, a flash of movement streaked across the dark sky, a low-flying transport skimming the terrain with no running lights. Its profile was too small to be military, too fast to be civilian. It banked hard, cutting engine noise until only a faint hum remained.

The transceiver beeped twice. Elias smiled grimly. "Friends of friends."

The aircraft flared at the far edge of the basin, landing gear digging into the sand with a hiss. Its cargo bay door cracked open, revealing a narrow interior lit in red. Two figures emerged, silhouettes against the glow, signaling with silent urgency.

Evelyn and Elias sprinted. The helicopter roared back overhead, its beam spearing the ridge behind them. Gunfire cracked through the night, distant but real. Sand kicked up around their feet as they ran for the open bay. One of the figures waved them in.

Elias dove up the ramp first, yanking Evelyn inside. The cargo door slammed shut behind them, and the aircraft lifted before they'd even found their balance.

Inside, the air smelled of oil and ozone. The two figures removed their masks. A man and a woman, both in plain clothes, eyes sharp.

"Reed. Mallick," the woman said. Her voice matched the transmission from the station. "You're late."

Elias steadied himself against the bulkhead. "We were busy not dying."

Evelyn's breath still came in short bursts. "Who are you?"

The woman tilted her head slightly. "The ones who listened to the stones while everyone else buried them."

The man in the cockpit called back without turning. "We've got two drones tailing us. We need to move fast."

The woman nodded toward the satchel strapped across Evelyn's chest. "That's it?"

Evelyn nodded.

The woman's expression hardened. "Then you're about to learn how many people would burn down the world to keep that from breathing air."

The aircraft climbed sharply, banking west toward the dark spine of the mountains. Below, searchlights combed the desert like the twitching legs of some hungry machine. The ravine where it had all begun faded into blackness.

They landed two hours later in what looked like an abandoned airfield carved into a salt flat. Hangars with collapsed roofs lined the runway. Only one structure had light: a long, narrow warehouse whose windows were painted black.

Evelyn stepped out, wind whipping at her hair. The air smelled faintly of metal and brine.

Inside the warehouse, the world changed.

Banks of servers hummed softly. Satellite feeds flickered across wall-mounted screens, each showing different points across the globe, ancient sites, restricted facilities, shipping routes. Maps were layered with spiral symbols.

A small group of people moved between stations, some in field gear, others in plain clothes. Not a military unit. Not academics either. Something in between.

The woman who'd pulled them from the desert gestured to a cleared space at the center. "We call ourselves the Orphean Network. That's not our name, but it's the one they use when they talk about us."

"They?" Elias asked.

She gave a thin smile. "The ones who bury what they can't control."

Another figure approached, older, tall, hair silver and eyes sharp with the kind of intelligence that sees too much. He didn't waste time on introductions. His gaze landed on Evelyn's satchel.

"You opened it."

Evelyn held his stare. "Yes."

"Then everything changes."

He gestured for her to place the codex on the table in front of him. As she set it down, the air in the room seemed to shift as if everyone present recognized the weight of what lay between them.

The codex pulsed once, faint but undeniable.

The older man spoke quietly, more to the room than to her. "For centuries, we've kept the spiral alive through fragments, inscriptions, oral maps, bits of what they didn't burn. What you found down there is the whole song."

Elias folded his arms. "And what happens when the whole world hears it?"

The man's expression was unreadable. "Empires fracture when their myths are shown a mirror."

Evelyn felt the room tighten around that sentence. The faces around her bore the kind of wear that came from years in the shadows. Some were excited. Some were afraid. None of them seemed surprised.

"You've made yourselves targets," the man continued. "The organization that's been chasing you isn't a faction. It's a consortium. States. Orders. Banks. Every hand that profits from a stable lie. And now, they'll come harder than they ever have."

Elias leaned forward. "Then we don't keep it hidden. We give it to everyone."

A murmur rippled through the room. Some nodded. Some frowned.

The woman who'd rescued them spoke next. "Broadcasting the codex isn't just releasing information. It's detonating a century of controlled narratives. You'd be giving power to everyone who can read, interpret, and weaponize it. That includes them."

Evelyn traced her fingers along the codex's edge. "Or we can let them bury it again. And this time, they'll make sure there isn't another chamber left to find."

Silence.

The older man finally nodded. "Then we do this carefully. The codex doesn't just carry text. It carries structure. Layers. A map to every point where truth was hidden. If we can unlock that, they'll never be able to silence it again. Not entirely."

A technician at one of the consoles called out, voice tight. "Inbound signals. Multiple encrypted channels lighting up. They know we pulled them out."

Elias turned to Evelyn. "We just became the loudest signal on the planet."

She met his gaze. "Good."

The codex pulsed again, steady as a heartbeat.

Outside, across oceans and borders, signals shifted. Old archives flickered awake. Hidden rooms and watchers stirred. Somewhere deep in a marble office, a man leaned over a phone and whispered, "They found it."

Somewhere else, in a monastery carved into the side of a mountain, in a vault beneath a cathedral, in a data center sealed under layers of jurisdiction, doors that had been locked for generations began to open.

Evelyn looked at the glowing codex, then at Elias. "This isn't about us anymore."

He gave a thin, sharp smile. "No. It's about everyone who thought this day would never come."

The world's oldest secret was no longer sleeping.

It was awake.

7: The Herodian Connection

The dry winds of the Levant swept across the tarmac as Evelyn and Elias stepped off the chartered aircraft. After their time in Ethiopia's highlands, the heat felt familiar, almost like a summons. The air carried the scent of dust and distant pine, a reminder that they were returning not to a resting point but to a beginning. The fragile parchment from Axum, carefully stored, had ceased to be an artifact. It had become a key. Its strange weave of archaic Hebrew, early Greek, and Ge'ez pointed them back to Judaea, to a time when cultures collided and new ideas took root in the shifting sands of history.

Their return was not retracing old ground. This was a recalibration, a narrowing of the hunt. The hills around Galilee and the Judean desert no longer felt like static ruins. They were alive with potential, a living archive waiting to be read correctly. From their transport, Evelyn watched the hills unfurl below them. For years she had walked these places with questions she could barely name. Now, the parchment had given them shape.

Elias leaned over a map spread across his lap. "That blend of Greek and Hebrew isn't random," he said quietly. "It's the language of people who moved easily between worlds. That puts us in Judaea, early first century. Somewhere in those scholarly circles, something was written that was never meant to disappear."

Years earlier, their work here had been broad and cautious. They studied synagogues, rabbinic fragments, Qumran and Masada. Now their lens was sharper. Ethiopia had changed everything. They were no longer looking for general evidence of early Christianity. They were tracking the ghost of a specific text.

Evelyn pressed her forehead to the window. "That older Greek dialect is telling," she murmured. "It's not just Alexandrian influence. It could be native Judaean scholarship. This wasn't a community passively receiving Hellenistic thought. They were shaping it."

Their first stop was Jerusalem. The city carried its centuries openly, each stone holding a dozen stories. The narrow alleys of the Old City buzzed with tourists, but Evelyn and Elias moved like listeners at the edge of a crowded room, waiting for a single note beneath the noise. They sought scholars who might know the odd corners of language, places where Hebrew and Greek had fused in the Herodian period.

At the Studium Biblicum Franciscanum, Father Michael greeted them with the weary curiosity of someone who had heard too many theories but still wanted to believe in one more. He had already heard whispers of their Ethiopian find.

"The linguistic fusion you describe," Father Michael rasped, leading them to a collection of papyri from Jericho, "fits the Herodian period. Hebrew, Aramaic, and Greek all coexisted. For the educated elite, fluency in all three was common."

He gestured to the faded ink. "Look closely. Greek philosophical terms in Aramaic text. This isn't mere borrowing. It's synthesis."

Evelyn bent over the glass. The shift between languages wasn't clumsy. It was elegant. "This is exactly what we saw in Axum," she whispered. "Thought expressed in two languages at once."

Herod the Great's court had been a crucible of this cultural fusion. A Jewish king with Roman patrons, a man who built cities with Greek theaters and funded temples he didn't worship in. He had surrounded himself with Greek scholars while claiming Jewish kingship. His sons continued the dance.

"This was an environment where language meant power," Elias observed. "And power leaves traces."

From Jerusalem, they turned north. The air around the Galilee carried the scent of olives and salt. Capernaum and its ruins lay quiet under the sun. A dig near an ancient synagogue introduced them to Dr. Ilana Cohen, an archaeologist with little patience for mystical claims. But the moment Evelyn spotted the pottery shards etched with archaic Greek lettering, Dr. Cohen's skepticism softened.

"These aren't Koine forms," Evelyn noted, tracing a letter's sharp angle. "This is older, almost pre-Koine, and it's deliberately preserved."

Dr. Cohen leaned in. "We thought they were just anomalies. But if this connects to your findings, we may be looking at deliberate use by an educated class."

Elias added, "The Herodian court, the priestly families like Caiaphas... they had access. If anyone was recording teachings outside the mainstream, it was them."

Their search led them into the desert. Qumran's silent cliffs still hummed with a kind of monastic defiance. In the archives, Evelyn found what she had hoped for: a sliver of text, labeled DSS 774. Barely legible, almost discarded. Greek diphthongs embedded in Hebrew words. Ligatures identical to those she had traced in Ethiopia.

Her hand trembled as she adjusted the light. "Elias. It's the same pattern. This isn't a descendant. This is the root."

Elias stared at the image. "So it started here. Not as an isolated Ethiopian text, but as something born in the soil of Judaea."

This changed everything. The Essenes and other desert sects had always been seen as marginal, separatist. But this text suggested something else: that they were innovators, forging language to hold ideas too complex for one tongue.

They turned to Masada next. The fortress rose against the evening sky like a monument to defiance. The wind up the snake path carried whispers of its last stand. Within these stones, they weren't looking for weapons or walls. They were looking for what might have been hidden when the end came.

"Masada wasn't just an outpost," Elias said, pausing by the remains of Herod's palace. "It was a refuge. If someone wanted to hide texts from Rome, this would have been a good place to do it."

The storerooms were still lined with the faint marks of organization. Evelyn ran her fingers over the rough stone. "These people prepared for a siege. And when people prepare, they preserve what matters most."

She imagined scribes hunched over lamps, copying a text they believed must survive even if they didn't. Perhaps a gospel written in Hebrew but carrying something subversive, something powerful enough that Rome would burn cities to silence it.

Her research turned next toward the Zealots. History remembered them as fighters, but revolutions are never just made of swords. Some Zealots, Evelyn suspected, might also have been scribes. Fervor could preserve texts as well as destroy them. The early Jesus movement and the Zealot cause may have brushed against one another more than scholars liked to admit.

"The language of this gospel," Elias noted, tapping his notebook, "is deeply Jewish. It's rooted in the Torah and the Prophets. But it's also messianic in a way that aligns with Zealot hope."

Evelyn nodded. "They could have seen Jesus as the liberator they were waiting for. Maybe not a warrior, but a Messiah who fit their vision."

The text's blend of Semitic structure and early Christian rhetoric made sense in this context. A group with one foot in armed resistance and another in prophetic expectation could have produced such a document.

Their undercover work took them into villages and marketplaces, slipping into the rhythms of daily life. Evelyn became Miriam, a quiet widow. Elias became Judah, a craftsman. It was in that disguise that they met Lysimachus, an aging Greek merchant with a private collection of forbidden scrolls.

He arrived cloaked, with one bodyguard, and a cautious eye. Evelyn's offer of a handwoven cloth opened the door. Talk of ancient stories kept it ajar.

"You speak of the First Ones," Lysimachus said slowly. "Not many care for such old currents."

Evelyn spoke softly, careful to let suggestion do the work. "My husband believed those words held truths buried too long."

Lysimachus leaned forward. "Some texts should stay buried. Others... are meant to be found only by those who know how to listen."

His guarded confession confirmed what they suspected. He owned fragments from desert sects devoted to a Hebrew-speaking Messiah. He called it "a fragile collection." They would need to earn his trust to see it.

Weeks later, in the hills, a woman older than memory herself whispered of a sanctuary hidden among the rocks. "They kept their words safe," she said, voice quivering like dry leaves. "A place of silence. Guarded by memory."

It wasn't a map. It was a direction.

The threads converged on power. The Herodian dynasty had patronized Greek learning even as they ruled a Jewish kingdom. Evelyn and Elias suspected that the rulers who tried to control the movement might also have preserved its words in their archives. A letter from a scribe named Nicodemus hinted at "writings that challenge the established order," locked away in the royal collection.

Jericho's Herodian villa offered their best lead. Its subterranean chambers had never been fully explored. Elias gained entry through a simple lie: a craftsman offering to repair pottery. In quiet corners, he noted walls too thick, spaces too regular. The kind of architecture that hid things rather than displayed them.

Their search eventually led to an ostracon from Tiberias, naming Antipas, a minor Herodian administrator, who had sought "the words of the Anointed One in His native tongue." It was the first tangible sign of a Herodian connection to the Hebrew gospel. In a private collection near Galilee, Evelyn found it inscribed on the base of an oil lamp, faint but deliberate.

"For the preservation of the words of the Anointed One, in His native tongue."

Evelyn and Elias exchanged a long, silent look. This was no longer just the work of sectarian scribes. It was a thread that ran through the desert, through revolt, through royal halls. The Gospel of the Hebrews was not a whisper at the margins. It was a current beneath the surface of a world that tried to bury it.

The Levant's night wind rose, carrying the grit of the desert against their skin. Somewhere in that vast landscape, the next piece of the gospel waited, wrapped in linen, hidden in stone, waiting for those who could still hear it.

Evelyn and Elias left the Galilee with the lamp carefully wrapped in linen, its inscription burned into their minds more than its clay. It was proof, but also a summons. The path pointed toward the hills where the old woman had spoken of silence and guardians.

The further they moved from the bustle of cities, the thinner the world felt. Villages grew wary, and strangers were greeted not with curiosity but calculation. Evelyn wore Miriam's identity more easily now. She had learned the rhythm of quiet speech, the weight of shared loss. Elias carried his tools in a weathered satchel, just another craftsman on the road. Their real work moved beneath every gesture, every false smile.

The sanctuary, if it existed, would not be marked on any map. It would be hidden the way all dangerous truths are hidden— in stories and silence. Local farmers spoke of old paths no one walked anymore, of caves that swallowed sound, of places where Roman soldiers did not follow. One man spat into the dirt and said, "Those who go that way don't always come back."

They reached the foothills under a sky smeared with twilight. Crags rose like teeth from the earth, and narrow paths cut through thorn and stone. At the base of one such rise, half swallowed by wild fig and dust, they found it—a dark opening, tall enough for a man to enter upright. The air that breathed out of it was cool and old.

Inside, their torches painted narrow walls with light. Carvings ran along the rock, shallow and weathered but still deliberate: Hebrew script mixed with symbols Evelyn recognized from the Axum codex. She ran her fingers across one line, whispering its translation. "For the day when memory must return."

The deeper they went, the quieter it became, as though the cave itself consumed their breath. At the end of the passage lay a stone chamber, no larger than a modest house. Clay jars lined the walls in uneven rows, some broken and crumbling, others intact, their lids sealed with resin long hardened. The smell of age filled the space—dust, earth, and the faint bite of something once living.

Evelyn knelt beside a jar and brushed away centuries of grit. Her hands did not tremble until the lid came free with a dull crack. Inside, wrapped in linen so fragile it seemed woven from air, was a scroll. Not Greek. Not Coptic. Hebrew—written with the same archaic precision she had traced in Axum.

Elias crouched beside her. "Tell me you're seeing what I think you're seeing."

Her breath caught. "This isn't just a fragment. This is a full text."

It was only then that they noticed the second passage of the chamber. Narrow. Almost invisible in the shadows. Torchlight caught a glint of metal. A spearhead. Roman. Someone else had found this place long ago—or guarded it still.

They moved cautiously. Every footfall echoed like a confession. The tunnel curved, and at its end stood a small alcove carved into the rock. An object rested upon a stone shelf: a leaden disc etched with constellations, nearly identical to the one Evelyn had once held in Ethiopia. She traced the pattern of stars with her thumb.

"They were connected," she whispered. "Whoever hid this knew the gospel wasn't confined to one land."

Behind them, a soft scrape of stone on stone. Elias spun, torch raised. No one. Only a gust of wind, or something moving deeper in the dark.

"This place isn't forgotten," he said quietly. "Someone has been here."

Evelyn carefully tucked the scroll into their satchel. They extinguished one torch and moved in silence, every instinct sharpened by the weight of what they now carried. The text was real. The Herodian connection was no longer speculation.

And somewhere in the darkness of the Judean hills, someone—
or something—still watched over it.

Outside, night draped itself across the land. In the distance,
torchlights moved along the Roman roads. Patrols. The time for
quiet scholarship was ending. What they carried now was no
longer just a relic of faith. It was a threat.

Elias tightened the strap on his pack. "This changes
everything."

Evelyn looked once more at the cave mouth, swallowed by
darkness. "No," she said softly. "It only begins it."

8: The Monastery of Silence

The Herodian connection had illuminated much, but it also left Evelyn and Elias chasing a ghost. Each new clue sharpened their vision while pushing the truth further away, buried in the guarded archives of a dynasty that had lived between Roman power and Jewish tradition. The whispers of Lysimachus, Nicodemus's veiled warnings, and Antipas's lamp were not random echoes. They revealed a thread of awareness among the ruling class, a recognition of the Gospel of the Hebrews as something too dangerous to destroy and too explosive to fully reveal.

Elias leaned over a table scarred with age, tracing caravan routes and ancient trade lines with a calloused finger. "The Herodian court wasn't just a seat of power," he murmured. "It was a junction. They traded influence the way others traded spices. If they knew about the gospel, they would have hidden it far from the grasp of politics and war."

Evelyn's gaze sharpened. "They wouldn't have locked it in a palace. Palaces fall. Power shifts. But monasteries..." Her words trailed into thought.

Their research, drawn from scattered archives, trade records, and half forgotten monastic chronicles, began to point toward a pattern. The gospel had not simply disappeared. It had moved, carried westward with those who fled the collapse of Jerusalem, passed through quiet hands into the shadows of early Christian diaspora. To survive the purges and the wars, it needed isolation, discipline, and silence.

They turned their attention to the remote sanctuaries of early Christendom, mountain monasteries beyond the political reach of empires. As the Roman world expanded, these silent enclaves became safe harbors for texts the empire feared or ignored. Evelyn's research narrowed the field to the Pyrenees, where fragments of legend spoke of a "repository of ancient truths," hidden high among inaccessible peaks.

Their journey began quietly. No grand departure, only the deliberate shedding of comforts. The bustle of Judea and Alexandria faded behind them as they moved north along trade routes disguised as merchants. In markets and caravanserai they listened, piecing together whispers about cloisters where monks spoke little but remembered much.

The further they traveled, the cooler the air grew. Forest replaced desert. Mountain passes rose like stern gatekeepers. In the foothills of the Alps, they met an old woman who spoke reverently of a monastery hidden "where the mountains listen more than men." She described monks who never spoke, who spent their days copying texts no one else remembered.

Elias traced their path on a battered map that bore the ink of a hundred forgotten roads. "This isn't a legend," he said. "It's a pattern."

Days of travel became weeks of pilgrimage. Each climb thinned the air, stripped away the noise of the world, and drew them deeper into the kind of silence only mountains can hold. When they finally reached the Pyrenees, the legends grew louder in their quiet way: a narrow pass, a hidden valley, monks who guarded something too old and dangerous for the outside world.

The path wound upward like a thread between stone giants. Winds howled, sharp with snow and pine. The final ascent was a knife edge, a goat track clinging to sheer cliffs. By the time the valley opened before them, dusk had set the peaks ablaze in crimson and gold.

Carved into the mountainside like a memory was the monastery. It was not a single building but a collection of stone dwellings and scriptoria grown out of the rock itself. A faint wisp of smoke rose into the cold air. No bells. No movement. Only the stillness of centuries.

The silence that surrounded the monastery was unlike any they had encountered. It was alive, listening. Evelyn's heartbeat seemed loud in her own ears. Elias, usually unshakable, hesitated before the heavy wooden door.

When it finally opened, it revealed a figure wrapped in a cowl of deep brown wool. No greeting. No questions. Just a steady, assessing gaze.

"We seek sanctuary," Elias said, his voice unexpectedly uncertain. "And knowledge."

"Sanctuary is not sought," the figure replied, its voice low and resonant, "but earned."

Evelyn stepped forward, her scholar's instinct guiding her words. "We are seekers of forgotten gospels. We followed a trail from Judea to this mountain. We believe something was brought here long ago, a gospel written in the tongue of the first believers."

The figure inclined its head. "Many seek what they cannot bear to find. Follow."

They entered the monastery, leaving the world behind. The corridor breathed cool air, smelling faintly of incense and old parchment. Light came from oil lamps, their flames thin and patient. A chamber opened ahead, and more cowled figures waited around a table worn smooth by time.

The Elder at its head regarded them in silence before speaking. "Few reach this place. Fewer still understand what they ask for. Tell us what you seek in our silence."

Evelyn spoke without hesitation. "A text, older than the canonical gospels, written in the language of the covenant. A text hidden when empires rose and fell."

The Elder's eyes were steady. "And if it is here, what would you do with it?"

"We would study it," Elias said. "Not for power. Not for acclaim. For truth."

The Elder let silence stretch like a test. "Truth is not a banner to wave in the wind. It is a burden. To carry it, one must accept its weight."

He rose slowly and gestured toward a shadowed corridor. "Then let us see whether you understand what you seek."

The scriptorium was carved deep into the mountain's heart, a cavern of whispers and flame. Oil lamps flickered against the walls, revealing shelves hewn from stone and lined with scrolls, codices, and fragments so old they seemed to breathe the memory of other ages. The air was thick with cedar oil and dust, but also something weightier, reverence.

Brother Theron guided them through the labyrinthine chamber with a calm that spoke of a lifetime spent in silence. His thin fingers hovered over ancient vellum as if touching it might disturb the centuries. "This is the Litany of Hidden Gospels," he said softly. "Not a single list, but a memory. Each notation is a whisper preserved by those who understood the danger of careless revelation."

He unfurled a brittle scroll. Its ink had faded to the color of dried earth, but its letters were unmistakable. Hebrew, laced with Aramaic, the rhythm of a language that belonged to the earliest followers. "The Gospel of the Hebrews," Theron said. "Or rather, the shadow it left here."

Evelyn leaned closer, her breath catching at the subtle cadence of the script. "This is what they carried with them," she whispered. "This is why they fled."

Theron nodded. "When power changed hands, the gospel did not die. It withdrew. The Church feared its roots. It spoke too directly, too plainly, of the Master as a man of His people, not a figure of empire. Some feared it would fracture their carefully built unity. So it was hidden, here among other dangerous truths."

He opened another scroll, its ink sharp and dark. "This is Brother Eliphas's record. Tenth century. He gathered stories from pilgrims and traders who whispered of a Hebrew gospel still breathing beneath the weight of official history. He believed it was not a single text, but a living tradition."

Elias studied the fine strokes. "A thread that was never cut," he murmured.

"Only hidden," Theron said. "And guarded."

They spent days immersed in the Litany, tracing faint lines through centuries of careful silence. What they found was not just a text, but the history of those who had chosen silence over destruction. Monks who copied in secret. Scholars who whispered their findings into trusted ears. Communities that carried a fragile fire through centuries of cold.

But the monastery's silence was not untouched.

The first sign was small. A jar of rare pigment, prepared for delicate restoration, was found watered down. A brush, kept in perfect order, bore a faint, unfamiliar mark. Tools vanished and returned. At first they dismissed it as the wear of old hands and older walls. Evelyn, however, began to keep a quiet record. She saw a pattern forming in the dust.

Brother Theron listened to her findings without surprise. "We have been targets before," he said quietly. "Knowledge draws shadows as surely as it draws seekers."

That night, Elias noticed Brother Matthias, the kindly gardener with soil under his nails and a gentle smile, lingering near the scriptorium long after vespers. A week later, he saw Brother Silas, a scribe with nervous hands, flinch when Evelyn spoke of the gospel's most disruptive passages. There was tension under the quiet. The Coil had found its way in.

The Serpent's Coil had haunted their research from the beginning, an invisible hand steering history from the shadows. Infiltrating governments, archives, universities, and now the last sanctuary of the Hebrew gospel. They worked not with force, but with small, precise corruptions. A faded line. A missing brushstroke. A lie wrapped in silence.

Evelyn found the hawk carved into the handle of a brush. Small. Deliberate. A mark of the faction known for subverting knowledge rather than burning it. Her pulse quickened as she held it out to Elias. "They're here," she whispered. "Inside."

They began their hunt in silence. Evelyn altered her routine, planting false trails in their research notes. Elias watched the monks more closely, learning the rhythm of the monastery. Each small test narrowed the circle. Each faint reaction revealed intent.

Silas trembled when the Gospel of the Hebrews was mentioned. Matthias disappeared into the lower levels, claiming to tend the cisterns. Anselm, the gatekeeper, asked too many careful questions about their progress. It became a game of shadows in a place that had once promised only stillness.

Then came the proof. A batch of their carefully prepared ink failed overnight. Theron's analysis found traces of a contaminant that weakened pigments with time, a sabotage subtle enough to ruin weeks of work without leaving an obvious mark. That was not the work of a clumsy novice. It was deliberate.

Evelyn's suspicions hardened. Matthias's quiet smile was no longer gentle. Silas's nervousness was no longer devotion. Somewhere among them, the Coil was listening.

She and Elias devised a trap. She whispered, just loudly enough for the wrong ears, about a coded passage hidden in a fragment. She spoke of a meeting point in the old grotto beyond the lower gardens, where the original copy of the gospel might be hidden. Theron arranged the monastery's watch quietly, without disrupting the silence.

The trap was set.

The night was clear, moonlight silver on stone. They waited in the shadows near the grotto, hearts drumming against the stillness. Footsteps crunched over gravel. A figure emerged, moving with the quick certainty of someone who believed they were unseen.

Matthias.

He carried a small carved hawk and placed it at the grotto entrance, a silent signal. As he turned, he froze. Elias and Evelyn stepped from the darkness, joined by Theron and the trusted monks who had kept watch for generations. Matthias's face was unreadable, his gentleness peeled away like old paint.

The monastery's silence did not break. It only deepened.

The Abbot's chamber was simple, its walls bare but for a single wooden cross and a shelf of ancient books. The late light of the mountain poured through an arched window, painting the floor in gold. Evelyn and Elias sat before the Abbot, while Theron stood behind them with the calm weight of history at his back.

"You have uncovered a truth that is both precious and perilous," the Abbot said. His voice carried not volume but authority, as if it had been shaped by centuries of listening.

"The Gospel of the Hebrews is not merely a forgotten text. It is a fault line."

He folded his hands. "In the right hands, it could illuminate the roots of the faith. In the wrong ones, it could break it."

Elias leaned forward. "The Serpent's Coil will not stop. They have already breached your sanctuary. Hiding the text will not save it forever."

"No," the Abbot agreed. "But neither will revealing it carelessly. What they seek is not the truth itself. They seek its control."

Evelyn met his gaze. "Then we take that control away from them."

The Abbot rose slowly, his robes whispering against the stone floor. "You have two paths. The first is to reveal the gospel in full. Translate it. Publish it. Let the world see what has been buried for centuries. The cost would be immediate. The Coil would strike. This monastery would burn."

He turned toward the window. "The second is to use the gospel as a blade rather than a banner. Within its passages lie prophecies and patterns. The Coil fears them. They reveal more than the text itself, they reveal the shape of their own design. You could help dismantle their network quietly, piece by piece, while the text remains here, untouched by their hands."

The room held its breath.

Elias spoke first. "The world deserves the truth."

The Abbot's voice was quiet but steady. "And truth deserves to survive long enough to matter."

Evelyn felt the weight settle in her chest. This was no simple academic decision. It was a moral fracture point. The gospel could be a torch or a weapon. But either way, it would draw fire.

"If we release it," Elias said softly, "the Coil will twist it. If we hold it, we become the thing we've fought against."

The Abbot's gaze softened. "No. If you hold it wisely, you become its stewards. This is not about keeping secrets. It is about keeping its voice clear until the world can hear it without those who would corrupt it."

He stepped closer. "So choose. Will you shout the truth into a storm, or will you use it to silence the storm itself?"

Evelyn closed her eyes for a heartbeat and saw the monastery's scriptorium, the fragile scrolls, the centuries of quiet defiance. She saw Matthias placing the hawk in the grotto. She saw the shadow the Coil cast on every archive and ruin they had touched.

"We dismantle them," she said finally. "Quietly. Thoroughly."

Elias nodded. "Then when the gospel speaks, it will not be through their mouths."

The Abbot inclined his head. "Then the burden is yours, as it has been ours. You are no longer seekers. You are guardians."

Outside, the mountain wind pressed against the stone, a cold but steady reminder of the world waiting below. The Gospel of the Hebrews remained in its chamber, untouched, unbound. For now, it would not be a rallying cry. It would be a blade in the dark.

9: The Map of Stars

The Abbot's chambers, usually a sanctuary of quiet
contemplation, had become a crucible for profound decisions.
The revelation of Matthias's treachery and the existence of the
Gospel of the Hebrews had thrust Evelyn and Elias into a
precarious position. Abbot Benedict, with his characteristic
wisdom and weighty responsibility, had presented them with a
stark choice: immediate and explosive revelation of the gospel,
or a more strategic and covert dismantling of the Serpent's
Coil, using the gospel's own prophecies as their guide. The
weight of that decision settled upon them, a silent promise of
the trials to come. They had chosen the latter, a path of careful
and deliberate action, to protect the monastery and to ensure
the gospel's truth would prevail uncorrupted by the
machinations of their enemies.

Their days since that momentous conversation were now a
blend of intense scholarly pursuit and heightened awareness of
their surroundings. The scriptorium, once a place of serene
study, now felt like a vital operational hub. Elias was immersed
in the linguistic nuances of the Hebrew texts, cross-referencing
them with ancient Semitic dialects, seeking the subtle shifts in
meaning that might betray deliberate alteration or a hidden
layer of interpretation. Evelyn, meanwhile, delved into the
monastery's extensive astronomical archives. Her focus had
been drawn to the Abbot's mention of prophecies within the
Gospel of the Hebrews that related to celestial events, a
concept that resonated deeply with the monastery's
fascination with the heavens.

It was within a dusty, seldom accessed alcove of the
monastery's vast library, a place where sunlight rarely
reached, that Evelyn made her discovery. Behind a false back in
a heavy oak cabinet, amidst crumbling scrolls and forgotten
theological treatises, lay a meticulously preserved chart. It was
unlike any astronomical map she had ever encountered.
Rendered on fine translucent vellum, the heavens were
depicted not as a collection of stars but as a tapestry of

interconnected patterns, each constellation delineated with both artistic precision and scholarly understanding.

The chart carried an unusual energy. It was alive with annotations and markings that hinted at celestial movements. Evelyn traced the delicate lines with her fingertip, her breath catching in her throat. Familiar figures of Ursa Major, Orion, and Cassiopeia were rendered with remarkable accuracy, but interspersed with these were symbols she did not immediately recognize. Celestial bodies were depicted with emphasis and pathways marked with delicate inked lines, suggesting not only static positions but journeys and conjunctions.

The script accompanying the chart was a revelation. It was a blend of ancient Hebrew and a form of Greek that suggested a pre-Mishnaic or early Hellenistic influence. The Abbot had spoken of the Gospel of the Hebrews as a text that predated much of the established dogma, and this chart seemed to be a tangible testament to that. The annotations spoke of significant conjunctions, luminaries in their proper houses, and the Great Sign. One passage, written in a hurried hand, seemed to directly reference a celestial event coinciding with a period of spiritual upheaval.

"Elias," Evelyn's voice, usually calm and measured, carried a tremor of excitement as she found him poring over a dense passage of the Hebrew text. She held up the vellum chart, its pale surface glowing in the dim light of the scriptorium. "Look at this. I found it in a hidden alcove. It's an astronomical chart, but more than that. It's annotated with something. I think it's connected to the gospel."

Elias's head snapped up, his eyes widening as he took in the artifact. He carefully set aside the scroll and approached Evelyn, his academic curiosity ignited. He examined the chart, his brow furrowed. "Remarkable," he murmured, tracing the intricate script. "The Hebrew here is archaic. And these Greek fragments are not incidental. They seem to contextualize the Hebrew terms, offering interpretation."

He pointed to a series of dots and lines that formed a complex geometric pattern. "This cluster here," he said, his finger hovering over a grouping of stars, "is depicted with unusual prominence. And the accompanying annotation speaks of the convergence of seven lights and the harbinger of revelation. This is not mere observation. It is tied to a narrative."

Evelyn nodded, her mind racing. "The Abbot mentioned prophecies. He said the Serpent's Coil feared the predictive passages most. What if this chart is not just a record, but a key? What if the Gospel of the Hebrews itself, or perhaps clues to its meaning or even its hiding place, are encoded within these celestial alignments?"

The notion hung in the air, heavy with possibility. The idea that ancient wisdom and spiritual truth could be interwoven with the cosmic dance of the stars echoed through many ancient traditions, especially within early Jewish sects and the nascent Christian movement. The Star of Bethlehem, the celestial signs interpreted by the Magi, all were traces of a time when humanity looked to the heavens for guidance and prophecy.

"If this is true," Elias mused, glancing toward the high arched windows of the scriptorium where pale twilight was gathering, "then our understanding of the Gospel of the Hebrews is incomplete without understanding its cosmic context. This text seems to be linked to the movements of the celestial bodies. It's not only about translating words. It's about deciphering a language spoken in light and motion across the vastness of time."

He turned back to Evelyn, urgency sharpening his tone. "We need more information. This chart is a piece of the puzzle, but we lack the context to interpret it. Who created this? When? And what events or patterns do these annotations refer to? The Serpent's Coil would understand its significance if they knew of its existence. Their fear of the prophecies suggests they understand the power of celestial foretelling."

The Abbot's warning echoed in Evelyn's mind: The Serpent's Coil has been tracking your progress. They know you are on the verge of a significant discovery. If this astronomical chart was part of that breakthrough, then its existence could place them in greater danger.

"We need to be discreet," Evelyn said, carefully re-rolling the vellum and placing it in its protective casing. "If this chart is as important as it seems, and if the Serpent's Coil is interested in the predictive elements of the gospel, then this could be precisely what they fear most. It is a direct link between prophecy and the heavens."

Their immediate concern shifted from the ancient text alone to its relationship with the cosmos. The Gospel of the Hebrews was not merely a document to be dissected. It was a prophecy embedded in the fabric of reality, its meaning illuminated by celestial clockwork. The ancient scribes had woven the divine narrative into the very stars, creating a map that spoke of both spiritual truth and earthly events.

Elias agreed. "The monks here are devoted scholars, but their expertise lies in theology and languages, not in archeoastronomy. If this chart is an astronomical key, we need someone who understands both the science and the history of ancient sky-watching. We need an expert."

The realization dawned on them: their pursuit of the gospel had led them to the threshold of a new discipline, one that bridged faith and science, history and the cosmos. They were not just scholars of ancient texts. They were becoming interpreters of the heavens.

The question of how to find such an expert without drawing the attention of the Serpent's Coil became their next hurdle. The world beyond the monastery's walls was a complex tapestry of alliances and rivalries, and the Coil's reach was vast. Introducing an outsider into their investigation could be disastrous. Yet without specialized knowledge, the secrets within the chart might remain forever out of reach.

"We cannot simply go to the nearest university and ask about ancient star charts related to religious texts," Evelyn mused. "That would be like shouting our intentions from the rooftops. The Serpent's Coil would intercept us."

Elias nodded, already sifting through possibilities. "We need to be subtle. Perhaps there are scholars who operate on the fringe, respected for their knowledge but not in the limelight. Those who study ancient calendars, forgotten observatories, or astronomical symbolism in ancient art. They often see patterns mainstream academia overlooks."

He paused as a thought took shape. "The monastery has contacts, even if they are primarily within religious and scholarly circles. Perhaps there are individuals within those networks with an interest in these subjects. We could inquire indirectly through carefully worded letters, posing as academics researching ancient methods of timekeeping or celestial observation. The key is to frame our inquiry without revealing the true nature of the gospel or this chart."

Evelyn considered this carefully. The Abbot had entrusted them with dismantling the Coil, and this required a level of cunning they were still learning to wield. "What if," she suggested, "we focus on specific astronomical phenomena mentioned in the annotated text? If there are references to a particular comet or planetary alignment, or a unique stellar pattern, we could pose our questions around that."

She looked at the chart. "The Great Sign mentioned here is not a standard astronomical term. It implies something deliberately named and recorded. If we can identify what that sign might have been, and when it occurred, we can use that as a starting point for our search."

The process would be painstaking. It involved cross-referencing the ancient star chart with historical astronomical records, identifying potential celestial events that might have been perceived as a Great Sign, and then finding scholars who specialized in that phenomenon. It was a detective story written across the sky.

"The connection between religious texts and astronomical observation is deeply rooted," Elias explained. "Many ancient civilizations saw the heavens as a divine testament, a way for the gods to communicate with mortals. Early Jewish mystics developed systems for interpreting celestial events, linking them to spiritual insights and prophetic pronouncements. The Therapeutae, a Jewish ascetic sect mentioned by Philo of Alexandria, were known for aligning their lives with celestial cycles. It's not far-fetched. It's part of that era's spiritual reality."

He picked up a quill, turning it between his fingers. "If the Gospel of the Hebrews was intended for a specific audience who understood these celestial connections, then its meaning would be unlocked not just by textual exegesis but by understanding the astronomical context in which it was presented."

Evelyn's gaze returned to the vellum. The delicate inked lines seemed to hold untold stories, celestial narratives that spoke of a time when the heavens were a sacred text read by those who sought divine knowledge. The gospel was not just a book; it was part of a larger cosmic tapestry, and this chart was the needle and thread that might help them reweave its true pattern.

"We need to begin by dating this chart as accurately as possible," Evelyn said. "The style of drawing, the pigments, the script itself, and the celestial configurations could point to specific historical periods."

Their work was slow and methodical. Evelyn documented every detail of the chart, noting star positions, constellations, and annotated symbols, trying to cross-reference them with known astronomical events from antiquity. Elias delved into scholarly works on the intersection of religion and astronomy, searching for any mention of similar charts.

The monastery's archives began to yield further fragments. Among old histories were references to a period of celestial activity interpreted by early Christian writers as a sign of divine intervention. One particular passage described a rare alignment of Venus and Jupiter, accompanied by a bright comet. It matched elements of Evelyn's chart.

"Elias," Evelyn called, holding up the fragment. "This elder speaks of a time when the heavens opened and showed forth the signs of the coming age. He describes Venus and Jupiter in conjunction and a comet blazing like a torch across the night sky. He says it was a confirmation of prophecy, a sign that the old ways would be illuminated by a new light."

Elias traced the chart with his finger. "Venus and Jupiter are often called the evening and morning stars in ancient texts. Their conjunctions are rare and striking. And a comet would have been a Great Sign."

He looked at her, realization dawning. "If this chart is depicting a verifiable celestial event, then we can pinpoint the time of its creation, and by extension, the likely period of the gospel itself."

The need for an archeoastronomy expert now felt urgent. They needed someone who could verify these celestial observations, someone who understood ancient astronomy well enough to confirm if such an event had indeed occurred, and if so, when. This was not just academic curiosity; it was a critical step in protecting the gospel from the Coil.

Their search eventually converged on a name whispered in scholarly circles: Elias Thorne. Thorne was a brilliant but reclusive scholar who lived in a secluded villa overlooking the Mediterranean, his home rumored to be both library and observatory. His expertise lay at the intersection of ancient cosmology and verifiable astronomical phenomena. He was exactly who they needed.

Evelyn wrote to him carefully, framing their request as an academic inquiry into ancient astronomical observations tied to theological traditions. Weeks later, a reply arrived. Thorne agreed to meet in secret.

The meeting was set in a secluded cove far from prying eyes. Thorne was a man of quiet intensity, his sharp blue eyes holding the weight of centuries of accumulated knowledge. He handled the chart with reverence, tracing its delicate lines with practiced familiarity.

"The artistry is exceptional," Thorne murmured. "The precision of these stellar placements suggests a sophisticated understanding of observational astronomy for its time. And this script... a blend of proto-Hebrew and early Greek. These annotations are not decorative. They are keys."

He spoke at length of how ancient cultures viewed the heavens not as a backdrop but as divine text. Babylonian astronomers charted planets as manifestations of gods. Egyptian priests aligned temples to the stars. Early Jewish mystics saw constellations as living symbols. "The Serpent's Coil," Thorne concluded, "would indeed fear this chart. It contains predictive power. If they understand these alignments, they understand when and where to act."

Thorne began meticulously cross-referencing the celestial configurations with historical records. "The Great Sign you mentioned is intriguing. The ancients often attributed immense significance to conjunctions and unusual stellar phenomena. If this corresponds to a verifiable event, it could anchor our entire timeline."

He pointed to a dense area of the chart. "This alignment of Venus, Jupiter, and a prominent star in Leo occurred precisely in the year we suspect. That means the gospel's context may be tied to this moment. And if the chart contains terrestrial markers, it may point to a location."

Evelyn and Elias listened as Thorne unfolded his theory. Ancient builders often mirrored the heavens on earth, aligning sacred sites to star patterns. "This chart might not just map the sky," he said. "It may mirror a place."

As he studied the more abstract symbols, he identified directional indicators, sequences, and what he believed to be navigational markers. "If this chart leads somewhere, these are the steps. They guide a pilgrim through a terrestrial landscape to a hidden point."

Their research deepened, shifting from scholarship to strategy. Thorne eventually located a site in a remote desert highland, a place rumored in legend as the City of Whispers. Its jagged peaks and a vast circular depression aligned eerily well with the chart. It was the kind of place where the ancients might have built an open-air observatory.

"If the gospel was preserved anywhere," Thorne told them, "it may have been here."

The desert stretched endlessly beneath a star-pierced sky. Evelyn adjusted the focus on the refractor telescope as Elias checked the vellum under the soft glow of a lamp. Thorne's calculations had led them to the heart of the circular depression, the supposed observatory.

"The alignment for the equinox is shifting," Elias whispered. "The Whispering Star should crest the eastern ridge any moment."

Evelyn nudged the telescope's mount. The still air amplified every sound. She felt the weight of the moment settle around them. Somewhere out there, the Serpent's Coil was also moving. This was not a race they could afford to lose.

"Lights," she hissed suddenly. Far to the east, a cluster of dim beams moved in coordinated formation.

Elias checked the map. "They're positioning themselves between us and the observation point."

The convoy of vehicles crept over the ridge. The Coil had anticipated them. Evelyn's heart pounded. "They're not just watching. They're here to intercept."

They moved fast, circling wide through the western terrain, abandoning their vehicle and proceeding on foot through jagged ravines. The Whispering Star rose above the horizon, casting a pale light over the depression.

"This is it," Elias breathed. "The markings match the terrain."

Evelyn focused the telescope. As the star reached its zenith, its light seemed to intensify and beam toward the center of the depression. A faint shimmer illuminated carvings on the base of a stone spire. Symbols etched long ago glowed softly in the night.

Then the radio crackled. Thorne's voice, tight with alarm, warned of approaching signatures. Before Evelyn could respond, a second voice broke through, cold and distorted. "Evelyn Hayes. Elias Finch. Surrender the chart and yourselves."

Searchlights cut through the darkness. Sleek black vehicles slid into position like predators. Armed figures emerged, disciplined and silent.

Elias's fingers flew across the chart. "The sequence... the symbols on the rock... they're a lock."

He sprinted toward the spire. Evelyn covered him, flashes from her camera disorienting the advancing agents. He touched the carvings in the order dictated by the chart. The first yielded nothing. The second made the ground tremble. The third brought a grinding rumble from within the rock.

A hidden door slid open, revealing a dark passageway.

"Go, Elias!" Evelyn shouted.

They fled into the darkness as the door sealed behind them. Outside, the Coil's agents shouted and pounded at the stone, their searchlights slicing the night.

Inside, silence pressed around them. The air was cool and still, heavy with centuries of secrets. They stood on the threshold of a hidden sanctuary, one that had been waiting for them since the stars themselves first whispered their story.

The chase had not ended. It had only just begun.

10: The Language of Symbols

The fragmented vellum, unearthed from its ancient resting place, was more than a collection of archaic Hebrew script. It was a palimpsest of meaning, layered with allegorical depths that Elias Thorne had only begun to glimpse. Evelyn, her fingers tracing the faded ink with reverence, felt the weight of generations of unspoken knowledge pressing down upon her. The Gospel of the Hebrews was not merely a historical artifact. It was a cipher, a carefully constructed edifice of symbols meant to be unlocked not through brute linguistic force, but through immersion in the consciousness of those who had created it.

"It's not just translation, Elias," she whispered into the lamplight, her voice soft but steady. "It's interpretation. The Hebrew itself is infused with a symbolic vocabulary that slips through the fingers like smoke." She gestured to a passage where the word for light was surrounded by small stylized figures that looked like seeds breaking through the earth. "Here, light isn't just illumination. It's germination. It's the spark of divine life, rising from the material world. And earth here isn't only soil. It's a womb."

Evelyn's grounding in ancient iconography gave her a sensitivity to the subtleties that others might have missed. She saw how the simple Hebrew characters were often embellished with flourishes that altered their meaning entirely. A single word for stone might have a curved stroke that suggested a mountain, or a cluster of dots arranged like a constellation, transforming a literal object into a cosmic metaphor. This was not a language for casual reading. It was a sacred lexicon, each stroke an invocation.

"Look at this," Elias said, leaning closer. His brow was furrowed, his scholar's mind alive with patterns. "Darkness is drawn here with swirling lines. It looks like water. And then there's this coiled serpent beside it."

Evelyn's eyes glinted in the light. "The darkness is not absence. It's the primordial abyss, the unmanifest potential. It's also the shadow of the divine. And the serpent is the force that stirs it into creation. It can mean wisdom, transformation, the cycle of descent and ascent."

The Gospel was threaded with dualities that were not opposites but partners. Light and darkness, ascent and descent, birth and decay, were interwoven as parts of a single living process. The text spoke of unfolding, often illustrated with petals opening, a divine flower revealing creation's breath.

Elias followed her hand to another set of illustrations. "These transformations," he murmured, "are rooted in nature. A serpent sheds its skin. A butterfly emerges from a chrysalis. A seed grows into a tree. This isn't poetic decoration. It's their grammar."

Evelyn nodded slowly. "They saw the divine in everything. It wasn't somewhere else, above or apart. It was immanent. Sacredness lived in leaves and rivers, in the pulse of breath."

She pointed to a passage describing a journey through a valley of shadows. The accompanying illustration intertwined sharp lines for shadows and soft curves for a path. The final letter of the Hebrew word for valley stretched downward like a well. "This valley isn't a metaphor for misfortune," she said. "It's descent. Into the world, into the soul, into the places where shadows live. The path shows how to walk through, not away."

Elias leaned back, thoughtful. "And the guidance here isn't overt," he said. "It's hidden in celestial patterns, in shapes of letters, in events of the natural world."

Evelyn smiled faintly. "Which means it was meant for initiates. People who already knew the code."

Her finger rested on the word for knowledge, intertwined with drawings of branching trees and flowing water. "Knowledge here is not fact. It's wisdom. It's the tree of growth, and the water of grace."

Near the end of the fragment lay a diagram: a central point surrounded by concentric circles, punctuated by symbols of stars, plants, and human figures. Hebrew words curved along each ring. Elias stared at it. "This looks like a cosmological map."

Evelyn tilted her head. "It's both a map of the world and of the soul. The center is the unmanifest divine. The rings are the realms of being. The human figures stand at the thresholds. It's a map of the journey inward."

The precision of the symbols spoke of an intelligence that understood the power of sacred geometry. To arrange words and images in these forms was to shape meaning itself. Evelyn felt the text breathing through the centuries. It was a living tradition, encoded in ink and pattern.

She touched a familiar symbol, an eye within a triangle. "This keeps appearing," she said quietly. "Always near passages on hidden knowledge. It might be the divine gaze, or the awakened gaze of the initiate."

Their work drew them deeper into the symbolic core of the Gospel. Evelyn spoke softly as she read. "The light is the essence that dwells in every created thing. This is a manual for igniting that inner light. The veil they describe isn't cloth. It's illusion. And when it tears, the world is revealed for what it truly is."

The text sang in the language of rivers, stars, and serpents. Each element carried more than one meaning, each image layered with cosmic resonance. The serpent in particular coiled through the text as a symbol of transformation, both earthly and celestial. It linked everything, whispering of cycles without end.

Evelyn paused, absorbing the interconnectedness of the imagery. "This journey," she said, tracing a spiral etched between two verses, "isn't linear. It's an ascent through repetition. A spiral of becoming."

The Gospel spoke not in simple declarations, but in layers that required the reader to shift between intellect and intuition. Evelyn often found herself silent for long moments, letting the meaning settle into her bones before speaking again.

"The darkness," she said softly, "is the womb of creation. It holds the seed of all things."

She pointed to a drawing shaped like an egg. "This is the cosmos before it cracked open."

Every symbol revealed another. The text was not merely a religious relic. It was a philosophical map of existence itself. The divine was not a distant presence but a pulse within everything. Light was not only seen. It was remembered.

Evelyn's eyes glimmered as she traced a recurring image of a river flowing into the sea, alongside the word for return. "This is the soul returning to its source," she said. "The river doesn't lose itself in the ocean. It becomes something larger."

Elias leaned over the table. "If Thorne's right, this text carries echoes of early Gnostic thought. The divine spark hidden in creation. The veil of ignorance. The ascent back to source."

Evelyn remembered her studies of the Nag Hammadi library. The aphorisms of the Gospel of Thomas, the mystical imagery of the Valentinian writings, the shimmering metaphors of light and unity. She heard them here too, beneath the Hebrew script like a low chord. The serpent coiling in the dark was not a tempter but a herald of awakening.

Thorne's hypothesis had always been that the Gospel of the Hebrews had been written for a closed circle of initiates. The deeper they read, the more certain she became. This was not a public sermon. It was a key.

Their discovery took a new turn the night they opened the old wooden chest in Thorne's private archives. Inside was a single scroll bound in the preserved skin of a serpent. The Codex Serpentis. Unlike the Gospel, this was not verse. It was a manual. A lattice of diagrams and glyphs, stark in their clarity. At its heart was the ouroboros, the serpent swallowing its tail, drawn with stars where its scales should be. Around it were lunar phases, constellations, and shapes of human spines, as if the cosmos and the human body mirrored each other.

Elias held it reverently. "This is the cipher."

The Codex mapped the heavens in an archaic style. Constellations bent and shifted, suggesting the sky as it might have looked centuries before the common reckoning. The diagrams corresponded with passages from the Gospel. A river of light beneath a crowned eye became, in the Codex, a celestial event, perhaps a comet or conjunction, shining above a symbolic spring labeled as divine emanation.

Evelyn traced a grid of symbols, each paired with a phrase and a number. "This is the glossary," she said. "Water is consciousness. Fire is transformation. The serpent is the force of creation."

The Codex described two serpents, one bright and one dark, entwined in a dance. Not enemies but complements. Their coils formed the pattern of creation. The serpent shedding its skin became a cosmic act. It was spiritual rebirth.

As they studied, a pattern emerged. The serpent was not only a creature of myth. It was a symbol for the pulse of existence, coiled in the world and in the human soul. The Codex suggested a belief in an immanent divinity that flowed through nature, the heavens, and human consciousness alike. The

Gospel was no longer an obscure text. It was a manual for transformation.

Evelyn felt the air in Thorne's library shift. Knowledge had weight, and they had opened something dangerous. Thorne's notes hinted that the Codex had been retrieved from beneath an ancient monastery in Anatolia. The men who had guarded it were not scholars.

The Codex's astronomical diagrams brought them back to the Whispering Star. Its triple halo, once a mystery, was explained as a celestial catalyst. When it appeared, the veil between worlds grew thin. It was a moment to act.

The serpent in the Codex coiled around a glowing point, labeled the divine womb. Evelyn's breath caught. "They saw creation as an embrace. Darkness and light entwined."

What they held was not mere scholarship. It was a living current of a forgotten tradition, and they were stepping directly into its path.

Beyond Thorne's circle, others were watching. A shadow organization had long sought the Gospel, but their interpretation was crude. They believed in a war between light and darkness, not in a dance. They saw the serpent as evil, the text as a weapon. To them, this was a manual for power, not awakening.

They hunted for battlefields where none existed. The valley of shadows, to them, was a physical location. They scoured maps for rivers and mountain crowns, while Evelyn and Elias understood the river of light as consciousness itself. Their enemies were searching for stones while they were learning the language of stars.

The Whispering Star, to the shadow organization, was a trumpet of war. To Evelyn and Elias, it was a bell of awakening. That difference was their shield.

Their adversaries clung to a God who thundered from above, blind to the divine that pulsed beneath their feet. They saw the serpent as a demon. Evelyn saw it as a mirror.

While the organization searched deserts, Evelyn and Elias sat in silence at Thorne's desk, tracing the curves of ink, breathing with the rhythm of an ancient script. Their opponents sought dominion. They sought understanding.

Thorne's meticulous notes had warned them that misinterpretation was more dangerous than ignorance. The organization's hunger for control had already led to destruction in places Evelyn had only heard of in whispers. They sought to possess what could not be possessed.

Evelyn read a passage about the veiled spring, a hidden source of wisdom. At first she imagined it as a distant place. Now she saw it clearly. It was within. It was courage when fear whispered. It was the reservoir beneath the doubts she carried.

Elias was silent, his eyes fixed on a passage about the unfurling seed. He was a man trained to question everything, to demand proof. Yet here, something in him softened. The seed was his own fragile belief, struggling against the hard soil of skepticism.

The labyrinth of echoes pressed on them both. It was not a place of stone. It was the noise of their own fears. Evelyn felt it when doubt crept in late at night. Elias felt it when memory reminded him of academic scorn. The text forced them to confront not only symbols on a page but the shadows in themselves.

The Silent Watcher appeared again and again in the margins, drawn as a figure without features, standing in stillness. Evelyn felt it as a presence, quiet and unwavering, watching her long nights at Thorne's desk. It gave her a strange sense of not being alone.

To Elias it was something else. A measure. A judge. A quiet proof that truth, if it existed, would stand on its own. Where Evelyn felt comfort, he felt challenge.

The Cosmic Weaver came next. An image of hands threading strands of light into the shape of worlds. Evelyn recognized herself in those hands. Every night she gathered fragments, weaving Gospel and Codex together into a coherent whole. She saw her own mind mirrored in the ancient image.

Elias saw order. Patterns beneath chaos. It became the symbol of his pursuit, the design he longed to uncover.

Evelyn reached a passage on the descent into the underworld. For her, it was the weight of secrecy and the strain of isolation. For him, it was the echo of professional exile, the memory of laughter behind closed doors. The Gospel had stopped being only text. It was now their mirror.

Even the celestial passages began to take on a personal shape. The conjunction of the twins spoke of dual forces finding unity. They saw themselves in that. Her intuition. His rigor. Two currents meeting to create something neither could alone.

Their work in that library had changed. It was no longer only about deciphering an ancient gospel. It was about deciphering themselves. Each symbol they traced on the fragile vellum seemed to speak both outward and inward, telling them what the ancients had known and what they themselves had always carried.

The Gospel of the Hebrews, in its layered silence, offered neither commands nor easy truths. It offered a language. It offered a mirror. It offered a path.

And as the lamp burned low in Thorne's study, Evelyn and Elias knew that the pursuit was no longer academic. It was a pilgrimage.

11: The Guardian's Betrayal

The air in the study had grown heavy. It was not the comforting weight of old paper, ink, and quiet work, but something far sharper. A prickling unease hung in the shadows between bookshelves. Professor Elias Davies had long been a pillar of their research, a scholar whose precision and brilliance made him indispensable. Evelyn had trusted him with their most fragile theories. He had authenticated key fragments of the Gospel, guided them through hidden archives, and opened doors that otherwise would have remained locked. He was the perfect ally.

Or so she had believed.

The shift in Davies's demeanor had not come as a violent storm but as a slow, inexorable erosion. Hesitations replaced confidence. Replies to urgent messages grew slower, explanations vaguer. Where once his sharp mind met every puzzle with unerring clarity, now it danced around the edges. Elias had dismissed it as workload and stress, but Evelyn felt the tremor beneath the surface.

The first undeniable crack appeared in the form of a small ivory box. Davies had acquired it from a private collection, swearing it was a rare artifact from the same period as the Gospel of the Hebrews. It fit too perfectly into their research, as though plucked from the past to illuminate their present. Then, one night, Evelyn found an auction record. It listed the exact same box, down to the smallest carving, with a different provenance. Davies's explanation was quick and smooth, but the trust in his voice was gone. It sounded rehearsed.

That discovery became the seed of doubt.

In the days that followed, Evelyn reexamined their entire history with Davies. She remembered how easily he had diverted them from studying a particular sect mentioned in the Gospel, calling it a scholarly dead end. She recalled moments when he had steered their attention toward certain interpretations and away from others. Elias, too, began to notice the evasions. He quietly asked colleagues about Davies's recent activities, and whispers reached him of meetings held behind closed doors. A name surfaced repeatedly.

Anton Vane.

Vane's reputation was a stain in the world of antiquities. He was a man who dealt in rare and forbidden objects, whispering to powerful collectors who valued secrets more than truth. If Davies was tied to Vane, then their research was no longer safe.

The betrayal took shape slowly, like an ink stain blooming through paper.

The real trap lay not in the archives, but in the Carpathian Mountains. Davies had urged them to relocate their work to a secluded research outpost. He had described the place as a sanctuary, a location with unique environmental properties that would allow them to analyze the most fragile fragments of the Gospel. He had spoken of security, discretion, and freedom from prying eyes. Evelyn had agreed reluctantly. Elias, despite his misgivings, had followed.

The first nights in the outpost were filled with a strange stillness. The locals avoided eye contact. Their movements were rehearsed. The silence did not feel like safety. It felt like waiting.

Evelyn noticed how Davies had insisted on one particular site, how he spoke of the coordinates with an almost feverish certainty. His reassurances now echoed with a hollow ring. Elias catalogued their supplies, checked their communications, tested the satellite phone, and found everything exactly as Davies had promised. Yet beneath the neat arrangements was the scent of a snare.

Evelyn was the first to give the fear a voice. "He's been unusually keen on these coordinates," she whispered one night over a map spread on their table. "It feels like he's guiding us to something. Or away from something else."

Elias did not deny it. The same pattern had begun to take root in his thoughts. Davies's obsession with the location no longer seemed academic. It felt designed.

The last piece fell into place when Elias found the journals. Davies had encrypted them, but not well enough. Inside were references to Anton Vane, to payments, and to "the package" being delivered at "the designated sanctuary." It was their sanctuary. Their supposed refuge.

Davies was not working for them. He was delivering them.

Evelyn's breath had caught when she read the entries. "He planned this from the beginning," she whispered. "Every artifact, every fragment, every coordinate was part of it."

Elias's face had hardened. "And we followed."

Midnight was the time Davies had chosen for their final analysis of the Gospel fragments. He had spoken with esoteric reverence about a thinning veil, a moment when secrets would reveal themselves. Evelyn saw it for what it was now. Not revelation. Entrapment.

They began to move quickly. Elias dismantled their equipment with the controlled urgency of a man who understood the difference between discovery and survival. Evelyn ripped the silver pendant from her neck. Davies had claimed it was an ancient amulet. Now it was likely a tracker.

The quiet of the outpost thickened into a suffocating stillness. The oak door was barred from the outside. Their caretakers had shed their neutral masks and stood as silent sentinels.

Outside, figures gathered in the treeline, their shapes too disciplined to be locals.

And then Davies stepped from the shadows.

He wore his tweed jacket as if it were armor, his expression calm, almost gentle. "Elias. Evelyn. I had hoped it wouldn't come to this."

Elias's voice was a low snarl. "You led us here. You did this."

Davies sighed. "It was necessary. What you're trying to bring into the world is dangerous. This knowledge isn't just history. It can unravel everything."

"Knowledge is not the enemy," Evelyn spat.

His eyes softened briefly, a crack in the polished facade. "Knowledge in the wrong hands is destruction. This is why there are custodians. They keep the balance."

Elias's jaw tightened. "You mean the people who buy and bury truths."

Davies shook his head slowly. "They protect the world from chaos. You've seen what's in that Gospel. Imagine if it spread. Faiths would collapse. Power would fracture. History would bleed into the present. Civilizations fall on less."

Evelyn saw it then. Davies did not see himself as a villain. He believed he was preserving the world. That made him more dangerous than she had feared.

"You betrayed us," Elias said.

"I saved you," Davies replied. "You'll live if you hand it over. I can guarantee that much."

Operatives moved closer, their steps measured, their eyes empty of hesitation. Evelyn's pulse thundered in her ears.

Elias reached into his satchel and pulled out the bronze astrolabe, the artifact Davies himself had helped them recover. With a single calculated movement, he hurled it into the nest of wires feeding the outpost's generator. Sparks exploded like gunfire.

The lights went black.

Shouts cut through the darkness. Operatives scrambled, disoriented. Davies barked orders. Evelyn felt Elias's hand close around hers. He pulled her toward the service hatch Davies had once described as a trivial piece of infrastructure. It was now their escape.

They slipped into the narrow tunnel as chaos erupted behind them.

The earth closed around them like a throat. The passage twisted and narrowed. Their breaths came in ragged gasps, their fingers trailing along damp stone as they pushed deeper into the darkness. The sound of pursuit echoed faintly from behind. They had minutes at best.

Davies's betrayal clung to Evelyn like a second skin. It was not the betrayal of a thief but of a guardian who had decided the world was not worthy of its own truths.

They reached the old ventilation shafts and climbed. The metal groaned beneath their weight. Voices rose behind them, closer now. Elias led them upward, always upward, until the tunnel opened into a vast cavern lit faintly by a slit of moonlight from above.

They crossed a narrow ledge. Flashlights flickered behind them. Shouts grew louder.

"Keep moving," Elias whispered.

They climbed through a curtain of moss into a smaller passage, jagged and ancient. The air smelled of stone and cold water. It led them to a roaring subterranean river, wide and black, its current fierce. It was both a barrier and their last chance.

They made a rope from vines and roots. Elias swung first, his boots skidding into the far bank. Evelyn followed. Her hands burned from the rough fibers, her heart hammering as floodlights flared behind her. Operatives spilled into the cavern mouth.

They disappeared into the treeline on the far side before the men could cross.

The forest wrapped them in its damp breath. The adrenaline burned itself out, leaving a hollow ache in its wake. Evelyn could still see Davies standing in the outpost courtyard, composed and resolute, as if betraying them had been his duty.

"He knew everything," she whispered as they crouched in the underbrush. "The tunnels. The river. Every step."

Elias turned to her sharply. "Evelyn—"

"I had to ask," she said, her voice breaking. "Did you tell him anything?"

His face twisted with hurt. "You think I would do that?"

The words hung between them like a blade. She hated herself for asking, but Davies's precision had been too perfect, his trap too tight. Suspicion was poison, but it was already in her veins.

Elias's jaw tightened. "He's a manipulator. He's had years to prepare this. He didn't need me to tell him anything."

She lowered her gaze, the weight of doubt pressing hard.

"We can't turn on each other," he said, his voice steadying. "That's what he wants. Divide us. Break us."

Her hand found his arm. "I know. I'm sorry."

The apology was quiet, but it carried the full gravity of their bond.

Above them the forest was vast and cold, its black canopy swallowing the moon. Below, Davies's operatives were no doubt scouring the tunnels.

They were no longer scholars on an academic quest. They were fugitives.

Elias pulled out a compass, its glass scratched but its needle true. "We head north," he said. "We find Thorne. He's the only one who might help us now."

Evelyn's fingers brushed the satchel at her side. The Gospel rested inside, silent but potent. Davies had called it dangerous. She called it truth. He wanted to bury it. They would set it free.

She looked at Elias, their shared exhaustion etched into both faces. "Let's finish what we started."

Together they vanished into the night, leaving behind the mountain and the man who had once been their guardian. His betrayal had been a blade, but it had also forged their resolve. The Gospel of the Hebrews would not remain hidden.

Not anymore.

12: The Path of Trials

The forest was alive with a quiet that felt too deliberate, as if the trees themselves were holding their breath. The night air clung to Evelyn's skin, thick with damp pine and unease. She could hear the steady rhythm of her boots against the soft earth, the quiet rasp of Elias's breath at her side, and somewhere beyond the darkness, the distant croak of a night bird. Every sound had a sharpness to it now. She had learned that silence could be louder than a shout.

Her mind wandered to Davies, to the precision with which he had orchestrated their fall in Rome. The betrayal was no longer raw, but it had shaped everything that followed. Trust had become a luxury, and in the world they now inhabited, luxuries could get you killed. Yet she trusted Elias. Not because he had earned it in some noble gesture, but because he had stayed when running would have been easier. That kind of loyalty was quieter and harder to fake.

"Thorne's address is in the antiquarian quarter," Elias whispered, his voice barely disturbing the damp night. "Old books, secret conversations. A place where someone like him can disappear without vanishing."

Evelyn scanned the tree line. "Or a place where Davies's eyes are already waiting."

Elias lifted a hand and they froze. Ahead, through the lattice of branches, a thin warm light flickered like a lantern on still water. It wasn't the white glare of a search party or a tactical unit. It was soft, amber, domestic. But that did not comfort her. Safety had worn that mask before.

"I'll check it first," Elias murmured.

"No," Evelyn said. "We walk in together. If it's a trap, I would rather see it coming than wait for it to swallow you."

For a moment they simply stood there, listening to the forest breathe. Then they moved forward, two shadows weaving through trees. The cabin appeared piece by piece, first its chimney, then its angular roof, then the glass of its windows catching the faint light. Smoke curled upward, slow and deliberate. Someone inside had been waiting.

The door opened before they reached it. A woman stepped out. Her posture was still as stone, her eyes unreadable in the lantern glow. No visible weapon, but the way she held herself told Evelyn she didn't need one.

"You are late," the woman said, as if they had arrived for an appointment that could not be missed.

Elias took a half step forward. "We came to see Dr. Thorne."

The woman gave a small smile. It held neither warmth nor hostility. "Thorne is not receiving visitors. But you were expected. Come inside."

The cabin was warmer than it should have been. The fire in the hearth gave off a low, steady crackle. Shelves lined the walls, filled with books that were arranged with almost surgical precision. No clutter. No carelessness. It was the kind of space built by someone who believed knowledge should be ordered, not discovered.

The woman introduced herself as Anya. She gestured for them to sit on low wooden chairs near the hearth. Evelyn lowered herself slowly, her instincts alert. Out of the shadowed corners emerged three more figures: an old man whose eyes glittered like mica, a young woman with ink-stained fingertips, and a large man who spoke with silence alone.

"You came looking for Aris Thorne," Anya said. "He knows of you. He knows of your work. And he knows what Davies hunts."

Evelyn studied her face. There was no sign of deception, only a calm certainty. "Then he knows about the Gospel."

Anya inclined her head. "He does. And so do we."

The old man leaned forward, resting his palms on a carved cane. "We are the Scribes of the Hidden Word. We keep what the world tries to forget. What men like Davies try to bury."

Evelyn felt something tighten in her chest. "Then you've been watching us."

"For some time," said the young woman, her voice as clear as glass. "Davies is only one piece of a larger machine. You collided with it because you were getting close to something that should have remained lost."

The large man finally spoke, his voice low and heavy. "We can keep you alive. We can give you the tools to finish what you've started. But if you stay, there is no going back."

Evelyn glanced at Elias. There was a flicker in his eyes, something between hunger and caution. "Why would you help us?" she asked.

"Because Davies has forgotten what we have not," the old man said. "Knowledge has its own will. If he buries it, it will find another way to rise. And sometimes it chooses inconvenient messengers."

Anya rose. "Follow me."

They left the cabin through a concealed trapdoor in the floor. A narrow stone stairwell descended into darkness. The walls were damp, breathing with the weight of the earth. When they emerged, Evelyn saw a cavernous chamber lit by oil lamps. Endless shelves of scrolls and codices filled the space, some wrapped in linen, others bound in crumbling leather. A soft, dry wind moved through the underground archive, carrying with it the scent of parchment, dust, and beeswax. It felt like walking into a living memory.

"This," Anya said, "is our refuge. And our burden."

The elder scribe rested a hand on a massive wooden table. Upon it lay carved ivory tablets etched with spirals of forgotten language. "You came to seek the truth. But knowledge must be earned. You will face two trials. If you fail, the truth remains closed."

Elias leaned forward. "What trials?"

"The first," the elder said, "is of understanding."

They led Evelyn and Elias to a low-lit chamber lined with celestial charts. The ivory tablets lay arranged like pieces of a puzzle. Constellations were carved into their surface with a precision that defied their age. Anya gestured for them to begin.

Evelyn knelt. She ran her fingers over the carvings, feeling the cold smoothness of bone. "These aren't just star maps," she murmured. "They're records."

Elias examined the text that coiled around the astronomical patterns. "There's grammar beneath the grammar. A code."

The Scribes watched in silence as the two worked. Hours bled together, broken only by the scraping of charcoal, the whisper of parchment, the rhythm of two minds meeting in a language no one had spoken for centuries. Evelyn's thoughts moved in layers. She pictured traders moving through Alexandria, monks scribbling by candlelight, heretics whispering ideas under vaulted ceilings. These tablets weren't a dead relic. They were the fossilized breath of a civilization that believed the stars spoke truths no emperor could silence.

She felt the shift when the pattern revealed itself. The constellations mapped to moments of rupture in human history. Empires falling. Knowledge blooming. Faith splintering. A cycle not of chance but of intention. "They believed the sky shaped history," she whispered. "Not just marked it."

Elias found an inscription at the center of one tablet. It was a single line, but it carried the weight of centuries. "The Great Recalibration," he translated softly. "A turning of the wheel."

The elder scribe's eyes glimmered. "Now you begin to see."

The second trial took them far from the archive. Anya handed Elias a small linen bundle. Inside was a strip of vellum with a cryptic verse.

"An amulet," she explained. "Forged by a scholar who once held the Gospel. It was hidden when the Scribes still believed in secrecy. Find it, and the next veil will fall."

The journey led them through long-forgotten routes. They crossed abandoned Roman roads, moved through a quiet monastery valley where the wind hummed like prayer, and finally reached the ruins of a mountain abbey. Time had hollowed it out. Walls were cracked, floors uneven, its chapel open to the stars.

Evelyn felt the place before she fully saw it. It was heavy with memory. She ran her hand over a stone worn smooth by centuries of kneeling monks. "Someone loved this place," she whispered.

Elias found the inscription first. It was carved into the base of the altar in an archaic dialect. The words spoke of a hidden star that revealed its location only when the sky aligned.

For two nights they waited. The wind bit through their cloaks, and the ruins sang with silence. Evelyn's thoughts wandered in the dark. She thought of the Gospel. She thought of Davies's cold precision. She thought of what it would mean to keep a secret so old that even time had forgotten its shape. Was she searching for truth, or something more dangerous?

On the third night the star appeared. A faint shimmer above the eastern ridge, almost too weak to notice. But the old lens Anya had given them caught it, and its narrow light fell on a single loose stone in the ossuary wall. Elias pried it free. Behind it was a wooden box, sealed with wax black as night. Inside lay the amulet.

Obsidian, cool and heavy, carved with spirals that echoed the celestial patterns on the ivory tablets. A single star gleamed at its center, catching the lantern light.

Evelyn held it in her palm. It pulsed faintly against her skin, a whisper of something older than any creed. She wondered what hands had hidden it. She wondered if they had felt the same shiver she did now.

When they returned to the Scribes, the elder received the amulet in silence. He placed it beside the tablets, his fingers trembling slightly. "You have earned your place," he said. "The Gospel will speak to you more clearly now."

But beneath the words was something else. Tension. Evelyn saw it in the way Anya avoided the elder's eyes, in the quick glances exchanged between the young woman and the silent man. The air had changed. The Gospel was not simply a treasure to them. It was a fault line.

In the days that followed, Evelyn saw the factions emerge. The Preservationists wanted to bury the Gospel deeper, to keep it as an artifact rather than a truth. The Pragmatists whispered of control and measured revelation. The Skepticizers questioned everything, even the right of the Scribes to hold it at all.

She lay awake in the dim dormitory one night, listening to the distant echo of arguments through the stone corridors. She thought of her father's voice, teaching her as a child to question everything she was given. She thought of the Gospel's quiet insistence that light belongs to all who seek it. She thought of Davies, who would burn every trace of it without hesitation.

Elias studied the factions with the cold precision of a strategist. "They're not a wall," he said quietly. "They're a cracked mirror. And cracks can be widened."

Evelyn stared at the amulet lying on the table. Its black surface reflected the lamplight like an eye. "If we widen them, what happens to the truth?"

"Truth survives," Elias said. "But who holds it changes."

Her pulse thudded in her ears. She could feel the shape of a war forming around them, but it was a war of whispers, not swords. Words could fracture empires. Secrets could topple faith. The Gospel of the Hebrews was not just a document. It was a blade.

She thought of the line from the Gospel that had lodged itself inside her like a splinter. The light does not belong to those who hide it. It belongs to those who carry it.

The Scribes believed themselves guardians. The resistance believed themselves liberators. But perhaps neither truly understood what they held.

The path of trials had brought Evelyn and Elias here, to a sanctuary built on knowledge and silence. But beneath that silence, a storm was gathering. And when it broke, it would not be contained.

Above the archives, the night sky was shifting. The hidden star that had once guided them through the ruins burned faintly against the dark, no longer a whisper but a quiet declaration.

Its light was steady, indifferent to who watched or who claimed it. Around it the constellations seemed to bend, as though something ancient had begun to stir.

Evelyn stood at the narrow window, the chill of the stone pressing against her palms. The factions below were already drawing their lines in silence, each convinced they alone understood the Gospel's power. But power had its own gravity. It pulled at everything around it until something broke.

For the first time, she felt it fully, not as an idea, but as a weight settling on her bones. This was no longer a search. It was a beginning.

She raised her eyes to the star, and something inside her steadied. "Let it come," she whispered.

The light did not answer, but it did not need to. It was already moving toward them.

13: The Revelation of the Hebrew

The scattered fragments of their search had finally resolved into a single, luminous point. The star charts, symbolic ciphers, annotated scrolls, and whispered testimonies of forgotten networks all converged on one destination. The chase that had begun as an intellectual excavation now pulsed with visceral urgency. The Gospel of the Hebrews was no longer a theory. It was near enough to taste.

Evelyn leaned over the star map, the pale lamplight catching the inked constellations. Each star, each line, each notation was precise. There was no randomness here, only intention. "They planted a trail," she murmured. "They left us a map across centuries."

Elias's eyes followed the constellation arcs. His finger traced the alignment that intersected three annotated coordinates. "This isn't just an astronomical chart. It's a route. Every pattern points to one place."

She whispered the name softly, as though saying it aloud might awaken something ancient. "The Valley of the Silent Watchers."

The Scribes had been deliberate in their erasures. Their influence could be seen not in what histories told, but in what they carefully avoided. Once, the Gospel had moved through the world like fire, igniting awakenings, fracturing doctrines, and shaking empires. Then it had vanished, buried beneath centuries of careful silence.

The coordinates were not symbolic abstractions. They pointed to a place carved deep into the bones of an unmarked mountain range. The old texts called it the root of wisdom. A sanctuary hidden in sacred silence. A vault designed to outlast kings and kingdoms.

They reached it beneath a moonless sky. The forest that ringed the valley was unnaturally quiet. Not the absence of sound, but something deeper, as though the world itself was holding its breath. The ground sloped downward into darkness. Time itself seemed to thin here.

Elias led with measured caution, reading the subtle cuts in the stone and faint, almost invisible etchings that only years of field work could have taught him to see. Evelyn followed close behind, her scholar's eye catching what others would have missed: the deliberate orientation of moss, the carved markers disguised as natural fissures, the order in the wild.

The valley resisted them at every turn. A cliff that seemed impassable yielded hidden handholds, invisible unless touched. A precarious stone bridge proved to be expertly engineered, sound beneath their weight. The obstacles were deliberate. They were meant to disorient the unworthy.

They reached a clearing ringed with ancient monoliths. Their surfaces bore weathered glyphs that seemed to shimmer faintly when touched by their lantern light. At the center, shallow depressions in the ground held smooth elemental stones. Evelyn felt the weight of the centuries pressing in. "This is a gate," she whispered. "Not just a marker."

Elias opened their satchel. Inside lay the wooden tokens they had carried for weeks. Each token represented a celestial force. Evelyn's mind moved quickly, matching token to stone: Sun to Light, Moon to Reflection, Earth to Stability, Spirit to the Spiral Bird, and Time to the repeating fractal pattern.

The last piece clicked into place, and the clearing inhaled.

A low hum rose from the ground. The monoliths flickered with pale luminescence, and the earth beneath their feet opened with the smooth, soundless motion of something alive. Cold air rose from below, scented with stone, vellum, and secrets that had waited too long to be spoken.

Evelyn and Elias descended into the dark.

The walls below were polished black obsidian, absorbing their lantern light until it seemed they were walking through the inside of a starless sky. Then the stone softened to opalescent marble that glowed from within. The air grew still, as though time had lost its urgency.

They entered a chamber vast and circular. Its walls were covered in carvings so intricate they seemed to breathe in the light. Star diagrams, figures of light, geometry spiraling outward like thought. It was not decoration but doctrine. A theology written in stone.

At the chamber's center stood a pedestal carved of luminous stone. Upon it rested what generations of Scribes had hidden and generations of seekers had dreamed of finding.

The Gospel of the Hebrews.

It was not one book but a collection of manuscripts bound in something smooth as leather and impossibly resilient. The ink shimmered softly, alive in the air. Evelyn approached with reverence. Her hand hovered above it, and the air around the text vibrated with a pulse older than language.

Her fingers touched the manuscript.

The world unfolded.

Light poured into her mind. Voices, languages, constellations, and memories surged through her like a river breaking a dam. She saw the early seekers standing beneath ancient skies. She saw councils and schisms, power bending faith into chains. She saw the Scribes turning away from the world to guard a light they believed the world was not ready to bear.

The Gospel spoke to her in a language older than speech.

Behind her, Elias whispered, "It's real."

"It's more than real," she answered softly.

And then came the light from the doorway.

Not the soft internal glow of the sanctuary, but the hard white glare of torches. Boots echoed on stone. Voices spoke in tight formations. Their hunt had arrived.

Silas Vance stepped into the chamber with the calm of a man who believed the ending had already been written. His operatives fanned out with machine precision, weapons gleaming faintly. The harsh beams of their torches cut through the warm light of the sanctuary like blades.

Elias shifted slightly, body angled between Evelyn and the intruders. His hand brushed the hidden device in his pocket. He did not need to speak. They had rehearsed moments like this in silence.

Vance's voice carried easily in the sanctum. "Professor Thorne. At last."

Evelyn met his gaze without flinching. "You're too late."

He smiled faintly. "For something this monumental, there is no such thing as too late."

His eyes lingered on the manuscripts as though they were already his. "Do you understand what you've unearthed? This is power. The kind of power that doesn't ask for permission."

"It isn't power," Evelyn said. "It's a mirror. And it doesn't belong to you."

Vance tilted his head. "Power belongs to those who can take it."

Elias moved first. A pulse of energy rippled from his hand. The torches flickered, and for a heartbeat, their formation fractured. Evelyn pressed her hand to the pedestal. She knew the sequence. The Scribes had built their final defense into the very bones of the chamber.

Light erupted from the walls.

The torch beams vanished into nothing as holographic constellations blossomed into the air. Symbols folded like living architecture, spiraling upward and inward. The sanctuary awakened.

Vance barked orders, his composure cracking. "Find them. Secure the artifact."

Evelyn and Elias melted into the chamber's shifting geometry. The Scribes had designed the sanctuary for seekers, not intruders. She touched the carved pattern on the western wall, and a hidden door opened like a whisper. Elias disabled one of the pursuing operatives with practiced precision before slipping through behind her.

The door sealed them away, muting the chaos.

In the narrow passage, the opalescent light returned, threading through the walls like veins of a living being. Evelyn exhaled sharply, but her mind was on fire with what she had seen. "The Gospel isn't just a text. It's a key."

Elias steadied his breath. "Then let's find out what it unlocks."

Her fingertips brushed the wall, and it responded. Lattices of light flared softly, forming patterns that shifted like thought itself. The corridor curved downward and opened into a smaller chamber, a hidden vault. Its walls shimmered with slow, deliberate light.

At its center rested a crystalline cylinder holding a scroll woven from strands of luminous material.

Evelyn stepped forward. "This is part of it. The Primer of Resonance."

Elias kept his eyes on the corridor but could not hide the flicker of awe on his face. "Another text?"

"More than a text. This is their guide."

The cylinder pulsed gently in her hands, its rhythm matching her heartbeat. She unlatched the seal. The scroll unfurled as if it had been waiting centuries for someone to touch it. The script shimmered in spirals and geometric arcs, not meant to be read in sequence but absorbed like a song.

Evelyn translated in a whisper. "The first principle is intention. The universe responds not to control but to resonance. To seek with hunger is to distort. To seek with harmony is to reveal."

Elias's eyes narrowed. "Then Vance will never be able to use it."

"No," she said. "He can only break himself trying."

The Primer spoke in luminous language. It described consciousness as a force braided into matter, not apart from it. It mapped the mind as part of the cosmos, not observer but participant. It offered not power, but alignment.

Evelyn felt something settle inside her as she read. The Gospel was not a weapon. It was a threshold. And they had crossed it.

Outside, the muted sound of Vance's operatives echoed faintly. The sanctuary was holding, but not forever. The walls pulsed softly, as if aware of the threat beyond.

Evelyn closed her eyes, feeling the scroll's light against her skin. "This isn't just knowledge. It's responsibility."

Elias nodded slowly. "And he's coming for it."

The scroll brightened as if in response. The sanctuary's geometry shifted again, soft lines aligning like a living star chart. The Gospel had chosen its moment. And them.

Evelyn opened her eyes, steady now. "Then let it come."

14: The Reckoning

The air in the inner sanctum, moments before thick with the hum of latent power and the scent of ancient parchment, now vibrated with a different kind of energy, the harsh crackle of discharged energy weapons and the guttural shouts of men driven by a single, brutal purpose. The temporary sanctuary Evelyn and Elias had found within the labyrinthine corridors had been shattered by the relentless pursuit of Vance's forces. The sealing of the passageway was a testament to the Scribes' ingenuity, but it was only a temporary bulwark, a momentary defiance against the overwhelming might of Vance's operation. They had anticipated pursuit, but not its immediate and violent culmination within the very heart of the Scribes' sanctuary.

Elias was already in motion, a blur of disciplined action. His energy pistol, previously a tool for exploration, was now a weapon of desperate defense. He had positioned himself between Evelyn and the encroaching breach, the narrow corridor offering a slight tactical advantage. The opalescent light, once a beacon of revelation, now cast long, dancing shadows that distorted the Scribes' intricate wall patterns into menacing shapes. Evelyn's heartbeat pounded in her ears as she clutched the crystalline cylinder containing the Primer of Resonance. Its gentle glow contrasted sharply with the violence around them. The Gospel of the Hebrews remained on its pedestal, a silent testament to the stakes of their desperate struggle.

"They're through the secondary seals," Elias shouted. His voice was strained, each word punctuated by the sharp crackle of outgoing fire. He ducked behind a raised section of the wall, the energy bolt aimed at his head ricocheting off the ancient stone with a shower of sparks. The Scribes' defenses, while formidable, were not designed for sustained combat against modern weaponry. They were meant to deter, mislead, and confound, not withstand a direct assault.

Evelyn pressed her back against a wall, her mind racing through fragments of the Primer she had studied. Beneath the chaos, a subtle pulse warmed against her chest. At first she thought it was her own heartbeat, but it was slower, steadier. The amulet nestled beneath her jacket was beginning to react. It pulsed once, then again, almost as if answering the violence with something older and deeper. She touched the metal through the fabric and felt it vibrate faintly. It was not fear. It was presence.

Driven by instinct and training, Evelyn moved toward a section of the wall adorned with a geometric pattern. She traced her fingertips across faint indentations she had cataloged earlier. As her touch followed the sequence, soft points of light flared beneath her skin. She remembered the Primer's passages on intent and harmonic alignment. This was not merely a physical structure. It was a system responsive to the will of those within it.

"Elias, the resonance," she cried, her fingers flying across the pattern. "The sanctuary isn't just stone. It's alive with energy. The Scribes built this to respond to more than force."

As she pressed the final symbol, a low hum filled the air, deeper and more powerful than before. The opalescent light intensified, thickening as if it were something they could touch. Elias saw the shift immediately. He adjusted his position, his pistol rising.

"What are you doing, Ev?"

"Redirecting the flow," she replied, her voice trembling but steady. "The sanctuary reacts to intent. If they bring aggression, it disrupts the harmony. If we counter it with resonance..."

The wall to their left shimmered, the air bending as a vortex of opalescent light burst into being. The first wave of Vance's men, caught off guard, stumbled as their weapons sputtered.

Elias fired a controlled burst into the distortion, not aiming to kill but to feed the phenomenon. The vortex pulsed and then snapped shut, stunning several of their pursuers.

"They're adapting too quickly," Elias barked. "Vance brought specialists."

The pulse beneath Evelyn's ribs grew stronger. She could feel the sanctuary's awareness. It wasn't a conscious mind, but something ancient and steady, like the echo of a thought left by a civilization that understood power differently. Her fingers moved faster. The patterns under her touch flared brighter. A wave of warmth pushed back against the encroaching chaos, and the floor beneath the advancing operatives rippled like water. Their formation broke as several lost their footing.

"Sir, the structure is unstable," a voice cried through a comm unit. "It's like walking on water."

Evelyn pressed deeper into the wall's interface. She wasn't building a barrier of force. She was generating dissonance, a counter rhythm. The attackers regrouped quickly, their advanced tactical gear absorbing energy rounds. Their helmets flickered with real time data. This was not a brute squad. This was a precision instrument, and they were closing in fast.

"They're pushing from the south passage too," Elias shouted. "We're boxed in."

Evelyn's panic spiked for a heartbeat. Then another line from the Primer surfaced. The resonance of shared purpose. This sanctuary was built not just to defend knowledge but to reflect the intent of those inside it. If she panicked, it would collapse inward. If she stood her ground, it would respond.

"Elias," she said, forcing her voice to steady, "project calm. It reacts to us."

He gave a bitter laugh as another bolt scorched the wall near his head. "Easy for you to say. They're shooting at me."

"Trust me."

He didn't answer, but his breathing slowed. He had always trusted her when it mattered. As Evelyn focused, the patterns in the wall brightened. The hum became a deep, resonant tone that filled the corridor and seemed to stretch beneath the floor and into the stone itself.

The ground beneath Vance's soldiers liquefied for an instant. Their boots magnetized to regain footing, but that moment gave Elias the space to lay down cover fire. It wasn't enough. They were too many. One section of wall shuddered. A bolt grazed Elias's arm. He hissed and returned fire.

Evelyn looked at the Gospel, still resting untouched on its pedestal. Its soft inner glow seemed to pulse with her heartbeat. This was why they had come. This was what could not fall into Vance's hands.

"There has to be another way," Elias muttered, scanning the walls. His gaze stopped at a section behind the pedestal. Stone receded with a grinding rumble. A simple, heavy door appeared. Not a hidden elegant archway but a crude, almost desperate fallback.

"It's a contingency," Evelyn said softly. "A way to preserve the Gospel even if the sanctuary falls."

"They're coming," Elias said. "Move."

She hesitated. Leaving the Gospel felt like abandoning everything. Elias grabbed her shoulder and shoved. "Take it."

She pressed her hand to the pedestal. The Primer flared like a living flame. The Gospel responded with a brilliant surge of light that blinded the approaching soldiers. Their optics failed.

Their comms went dead. For a breathless moment the sanctum belonged to no one but the Scribes and the echoes they had left behind.

Elias turned, his pistol roaring a last line of defense. Evelyn clutched the Gospel and the Primer and ran through the passage. The door ground closed behind her with the sound of finality. She heard his shouts. Then silence.

Her legs shook as she pushed deeper into the narrow corridor. The sound of distant pursuit echoed through the stone. Tears blurred her vision but did not slow her. The amulet pulsed now with every step. It was not passive. It was awake.

Somewhere ahead, Silas appeared like a shadow peeled from the wall. His robes were torn and his face ashen. He stumbled toward her, breathless and ragged. "Evelyn."

She spun, weapon half raised. "Why are you here?"

"I escaped," he rasped. "Vance doesn't need me anymore. But I know the way out."

Her grief churned with suspicion. "You led them here."

"I know," he whispered. "And I can't undo that. But I can help you survive. There's a passage he won't follow."

The amulet grew hotter. The tunnels narrowed. She followed him because there was nothing else to do.

As they moved, Silas began to speak in halting sentences about the last defense the Scribes had left. "There's a veil ahead," he said. "They built it for those they deemed worthy. Not all can pass."

Evelyn didn't answer. The Primer pulsed against her skin like a second heart. The warmth no longer felt neutral. It was a summons. The air thickened as they turned a final corner.

The shimmer appeared ahead of them. At first it was no more than a wavering in the air, like heat rising from stone. Then it resolved into concentric patterns, light breathing in and out. The floor beneath her boots vibrated faintly, as if an unseen heartbeat echoed through the stone.

Silas stopped short. "This is it."

Evelyn studied the veil. It wasn't just light. It was presence. Something vast and old seemed to be waiting on the other side. She touched the Primer. It flared in response, its lines of light threading across her palm like veins of fire. The shimmer rippled.

"It won't let everyone through," Silas said quietly.

"What about you?"

He didn't meet her eyes. "I cannot pass."

The admission was almost a confession. He took a step back, the weight of guilt pressing his shoulders down. "I have already failed their measure."

Her voice hardened. "Then why bring me here?"

"Because it will let you," he said. "Because if Vance gets the Gospel, everything we are becomes ash."

Boots echoed far behind them, slow and deliberate. The hunters were close.

Evelyn closed her eyes. For a heartbeat she saw Elias leaning over the map table, his steady hand tracing a line she now stood upon. This is the last place they cannot follow, he had said once. It isn't built for soldiers. It's built for those who carry the weight of knowing.

She opened her eyes. The shimmer pulsed. The Primer burned warm and steady. She stripped herself down to the core of what mattered. Not the chase. Not Vance. Not the betrayal. Only purpose.

The veil thickened into a lattice of gold and black. A low tone filled the chamber, deeper than anything she had ever heard. It vibrated through bone. She stepped forward. The air resisted her like water but then parted.

Heat and light coiled around her. She felt the ground fall away. Time stretched. The Primer's pulse matched her own. Images flickered through her vision: star maps drawn in living fire, faces she could not name, voices layered in strange harmonies. A single presence loomed at the edge of perception, vast and silent. It was not hostile. It was watching.

The lattice folded around her like a cocoon and then let go. She stumbled forward onto solid ground. Cold air cut across her face. The shimmer closed behind her with a sound like a sigh. Silas was gone. Vance's men would never follow.

She stood on a plateau under a sky scattered with sharp stars. The amulet cooled but did not return to silence. A faint pulse still aligned with her heartbeat, as though something on the other side of the veil had marked her. The wind rolled across the stone like a slow tide. She pressed a hand to the ground and felt it hum faintly, echoing the pulse inside her.

"Elias," she whispered. "I will not fail."

She descended the rocky slope, the night air filled with pine and damp earth. Each step away from the veil made the world feel more real. Yet something in her had shifted. The Primer had chosen her. The sanctuary had acknowledged her. The Gospel weighed heavily in her pack but it no longer felt like an artifact. It felt alive.

When the chapel came into view, its lanterns flickering faintly in the darkness, a figure emerged from the threshold. A woman with a hood pulled low stepped forward. Evelyn recognized her as one of the Circle's contacts, part of the resistance that had been working in the shadows to counter Vance's network.

"You made it," the woman said softly, her voice hushed as if afraid of breaking something fragile. Her eyes fell on the Primer. "And it chose you."

Evelyn said nothing at first. She felt the hum beneath her skin. She saw the shimmer still in the distance, faint like a memory burned into the night. Her grief for Elias sat like a stone behind her ribs, heavy and real. But beneath it was something new. Resolve.

"They'll come," Evelyn finally said.

The woman nodded. "Then we'll be ready."

Evelyn stepped inside the chapel. Its walls smelled of old wood and wax. The faint, rhythmic pulse of the Primer matched the candlelight flicker, as though it had been waiting here too. She felt eyes on her, not just from the people gathered but from something older that lived in the spaces between walls and time.

She did not look back at the veil. She didn't need to. It would always be there, waiting. And something on the other side was watching.

15: The Dawn of Truth

The air in the clandestine safe house, a stark contrast to the hushed reverence of the sanctuary vault, throbbed with a different kind of energy, one sharpened by purpose and sleepless intensity. Hidden beneath a decaying façade of a long-abandoned monastery outside Florence, the place had been reinforced over the years by the resistance, scholars, archivists, and quiet dissenters who had spent decades chipping at the edges of Vance's historical empire. Now, it had become something more: a nerve center. The Gospel of the Hebrews, bound in its faded vellum and sealed with the faint scent of time, lay upon a heavy wooden table in the center of the main room like a living thing.

The flickering lamplight cast warm halos over the manuscript's surface. Even in silence, it commanded attention. Evelyn stood at the edge of the table, fingers hovering just above the text, not quite touching. She could still feel the faint resonance of the amulet beneath her collarbone, that low hum that had begun in the sanctuary and never entirely faded. It matched the quiet, rhythmic thrum in the room, the sound of generators and servers humming in their hidden alcoves, of minds working with tireless urgency.

Around her, the resistance was in full motion. They had always worked in fragments and shadows, safeguarding truths that history's gatekeepers sought to bury. But tonight, there was a cohesion she had never witnessed before. Thorne's deep voice rumbled as he set up the scanning array, a machine that looked like a marriage between medieval craftsmanship and cutting-edge imaging technology. Anya sat cross-legged on the floor, surrounded by dictionaries, lexicons, and notebooks, her quick, precise hands sketching linguistic trees on yellow paper. Elias stood near the server racks, monitoring secure data streams, intercepting bursts of chatter already hinting that Vance's network knew something had slipped beyond its grasp.

"This is the moment they can't control," Elias said quietly.

Evelyn looked up. "Not yet. But they will try."

He nodded, his expression unreadable. He had been steady through the flight, the Threshold, the chapel, always assessing, always several moves ahead. But now she could see it in him too: a flicker of awe, quickly buried beneath calculation.

Thorne approached the table, his weathered hands careful as he adjusted his glasses. "The vellum is unlike anything I've seen outside the oldest Dead Sea Scrolls. The texture alone is remarkable. It feels alive."

"It is alive," Anya said, half distracted by her notes. "Words can be alive. They just need to be read."

She lifted one of the portable magnification lenses and leaned close to the illuminated text. "Look at this structure here. These ligatures aren't standard late Aramaic. They're transitional, almost like an intentional bridge between dialects. The Scribes must have known they were preserving something meant to outlast linguistic decay."

"Or they were hiding something in plain sight," Thorne murmured. "Language can be a vault as much as a key."

Evelyn exhaled slowly. The tension in her chest was a wire drawn tight. In that moment, the Gospel did not feel like an artifact. It felt like an obligation.

The days that followed blurred together in the rhythm of translation and surveillance. While Thorne and Anya dove into the text line by line, Elias and Evelyn coordinated secure transmissions, digital archiving, and preparations for the inevitable storm.

Each passage revealed more than history; it revealed intention. The Jesus described within was not the untouchable figurehead of Vance's carefully polished mythology but a man immersed in the living currents of Jewish mysticism, a rabbi and healer whose spiritual authority emerged from insight, not imperial sanction. His dialogues with Essene mystics were not framed as divine proclamations but as intellectual exchange. His parables resonated with the sound of a world still rooted in its covenant with its own ancestral faith.

"It reads like a conversation that never ended," Anya said one night, exhaustion and exhilaration written equally across her face. "Like something unfinished. Like they expected others to continue it."

"Or feared what would happen if it fell into the wrong hands," Thorne added gravely.

The Gospel's existence could not remain secret forever. The resistance had anticipated that. A controlled release was planned: authenticated fragments, high resolution scans, linguistic breakdowns, theological commentary. It was the culmination of months of theoretical planning, now suddenly real.

Evelyn stood over the central console as Elias keyed in the final encryption string. "Once this goes out, it can't be undone," he said.

"Good," she replied. "Then it will finally belong to everyone."

He glanced at her, something soft and fierce flickering in his eyes. "Are you ready for the war that follows?"

"No," she admitted. "But we've already been fighting it. This just moves it out of the shadows."

He pressed the key. The encrypted data surged into the digital ether, disseminated through academic mirrors, encrypted peer networks, and a dozen anonymous caches on dark servers and whistleblower archives.

For a moment, nothing happened. Then the room came alive. Notifications bloomed across their screens. Journalists in London and New York received fragments. Trusted academics in Jerusalem and Berlin decrypted their copies. A group of independent archivists in Buenos Aires mirrored the files before the sun rose on their side of the world.

The Gospel of the Hebrews was free.

The reaction came like a wave breaking across continents.

Theologians convened emergency roundtables. Denominational leaders issued statements that dripped with both fear and defiance. Vance's affiliated media networks deployed prepackaged talking points, the speed of their response confirming what Evelyn had always suspected: they had known such a text existed.

Bishops thundered in pulpits, calling the manuscript a blasphemous fabrication. Rabbinical scholars, more measured, debated its historical layers with cautious fascination. Secular academics saw in it a fissure that might reshape centuries of narrative scaffolding.

Public reaction was fiercer still. In Cairo, underground forums translated and reposted passages overnight. In Rome, televised debates stretched into dawn, theologians hurling accusations across glossy sets. In rural Kansas, preachers held revival meetings denouncing what they called the Heresy of the Hebrews. In Berlin, university students gathered outside the old library, candles in hand, reading aloud translations in the rain.

And in one quiet room beneath Florence, Evelyn listened to all of it, the sound of a world shifting.

"This is bigger than we imagined," Elias said, standing over the monitoring screen.

"It was always going to be," she answered.

Vance's counterattack was as swift as it was elegant.

Articles began to appear within hours, polished, rehearsed, dripping with calculated skepticism. Editorials accused Thorne of manufacturing evidence to resurrect his fading career. Anya was painted as a reckless idealist, seduced by conspiratorial fringe movements. Evelyn's name surfaced in a fabricated financial scandal that appeared in three separate outlets at once.

"They had this ready," Elias said grimly. "They've been waiting for this moment."

"They're trying to discredit us before the story matures," she said. "Classic suppression playbook. They control perception, they control the outcome."

But the Gospel was no longer a fragile secret. It was multiplying. Independent labs were already verifying ink and vellum age. Linguists were arguing over syntax in real time. A coalition of small but vocal academics was rising in defense.

"They underestimated how much people wanted a crack in the wall," Evelyn said.

The following week was an endless procession of screens, debates, statements, and silent hours at the table with the manuscript. Evelyn read by lamplight long after the others slept. She traced the lines not with her fingers but with her thoughts, following the shape of words written by hands long turned to dust.

She thought of Elias beside her in the sanctum, the sound of gunfire fading behind them. She thought of Silas and the Threshold, of the starry lattice that had judged and allowed her passage. She felt the hum of the amulet against her chest, now almost imperceptible but never gone.

This was not the end. This was the opening movement of something larger.

The world began to fracture along fault lines old and new.

Progressive theologians called the Gospel a bridge, a restoration of Jesus within Judaism, a chance to heal two millennia of division. Evangelical leaders labeled it heresy, a tool of Satan to weaken faith. Governments with strong religious identities issued official condemnations. Others quietly convened commissions of historians.

In Tel Aviv, a group of archivists began cross referencing obscure Essene texts with the newly released manuscript. In Geneva, a private consortium of museums petitioned for the right to house the original. In Washington, Vance's allies in government initiated a series of opaque investigations.

In every corner, the ground shifted.

Late one evening, Evelyn stepped out onto the crumbling stone balcony overlooking the hills. Florence slept beneath a soft mist. Her thoughts did not.

Elias joined her a moment later. He carried a cup of coffee he had forgotten to drink. "You're not sleeping."

"Neither are you."

He set the cup down. "Do you realize what we've done?"

She laughed softly. "You're asking me that now?"

He leaned against the railing, looking not at the city but at the horizon beyond. "We've cut a hole in the fabric of what people thought was settled. For some, it will be revelation. For others, betrayal."

"For Vance, it's war."

"For Vance, it's about control. He can lose the text, but he can't afford to lose the narrative."

Evelyn closed her eyes for a moment. "We have to be careful. If this turns into just another ideological war, the Gospel will become a weapon, not a key."

Elias nodded. "Which means we need to stay ahead of the story. We need allies. Real ones. Scholars. Faith leaders who are willing to confront what this means."

"We need more than that," she said quietly. "We need to understand why they buried this in the first place. If this was just the beginning of what they silenced, then we've only scratched the surface."

A few nights later, their network intercepted a communication buried deep within Vance's encrypted channels. The message contained no names, no explicit reference to the Gospel. But Evelyn recognized the codename embedded in the metadata.

Corona Spinea.

Latin. Crown of Thorns.

She felt the chill crawl up her spine before she spoke. "They're looking for something else."

Elias leaned over her shoulder. His eyes narrowed at the terminal. "So the Gospel wasn't the endgame."

"No," she whispered. "It was the lock. The Crown might be the key."

They stared at the screen in silence. Vance's network was already moving, quietly and methodically. Whatever lay beneath that name, it had been there long before the Gospel surfaced.

And that was when Evelyn understood. Their war had never been about one manuscript. It was about the architecture of hidden truths, constructed and buried piece by piece across centuries.

"This isn't over," Elias said.

"It's just beginning."

The months that followed were both exhilarating and dangerous. Academic institutions fractured along ideological lines. Some embraced the Gospel as a long-lost bridge between faiths. Others denounced it as corrosive heresy. Vance's organization, though wounded, moved with predatory intelligence. Disinformation blurred into legitimate debate, making it harder to tell friend from foe.

Thorne and Anya became household names in academic circles. Both wore the weight uneasily. "We didn't sign up to become icons," Anya admitted one evening. "We signed up to tell the truth."

"And now telling the truth has consequences," Thorne replied.

Evelyn and Elias grew quieter as the storm expanded. Their work became less about proving the Gospel's authenticity and more about preserving it from being co-opted or erased again. They built redundancies into their network, off grid archives, encrypted data vaults scattered across continents.

But even as they built, they listened. And the whispers grew louder. Corona Spinea appeared in more intercepted chatter. Black market artifact dealers in Istanbul. A Vatican archivist under quiet surveillance. An archaeological dig in Galilee sealed without explanation. The threads pointed to something buried deep in the intersection of faith, power, and fear.

Elias stared at the growing map of connections one night. "If the Gospel was meant to reframe the past, the Crown might be meant to control the future."

Evelyn didn't answer. She didn't need to.

The final night of that first long winter after the release of the Gospel, Evelyn returned alone to the manuscript table. The lamps burned low. The room was silent except for the rhythmic click of distant servers. She laid her palm against the vellum and closed her eyes.

The hum from the amulet beneath her collarbone answered her touch. For the first time since the Threshold, it flared faintly, a warmth that was neither warning nor comfort.

"This isn't where it ends," she whispered.

She opened her eyes to the quiet room and the world that waited beyond it. Vance's empire would regroup. The resistance would grow. And somewhere out there, buried in forgotten vaults and whispered in encrypted channels, the Crown of Thorns waited to be found.

Outside, dawn bled slowly across the Tuscan hills. The sky glowed with the muted colors of a world on the edge of a new epoch. Evelyn stood by the window as Elias joined her. Neither spoke. The silence between them was not uncertainty. It was readiness.

The Gospel had been the first strike. The Crown would be the next war.

Key Terms

The appendix provides supplementary material essential for a comprehensive understanding of the Gospel of the Hebrews and its historical context.

Transcriptions of Key Passages: Selected pivotal verses from the Gospel of the Hebrews, presented in their original Aramaic and a contemporary English translation, allowing for direct engagement with the text.

Comparative Analysis Charts: Tables that highlight significant thematic and doctrinal parallels and divergences between the Gospel of the Hebrews and other contemporary early Christian and Jewish texts, such as the Gospels of Matthew, Mark, Luke, John, and select Dead Sea Scrolls fragments.

Historical Timeline: A detailed chronological outline of key events, figures, and textual discoveries relevant to the emergence and reception of the Gospel of the Hebrews, spanning from the 1st century CE to the present day.

Genealogical Chart: A visual representation of the lineage of key figures discussed in the text, offering clarity on familial and historical connections that influenced the development of early religious thought.

This glossary defines terms and concepts central to the study of the Gospel of the Hebrews and its historical milieu.

Aramaic: An ancient Semitic language that served as a lingua franca in the Near East for many centuries and is believed to be the original language of the Gospel of the Hebrews.

Canon: The collection of books that are recognized as divinely inspired and authoritative in matters of faith and practice by a religious community.

Gospel: In Christian tradition, a narrative account of the life, teachings, death, and resurrection of Jesus Christ.

Heresy: A belief or theory that is strongly at variance with established beliefs or customs, particularly the accepted beliefs of a church or religious organization.

Midrash: A method of biblical interpretation that involves seeking out the deeper meaning or homiletic exposition of scripture.

Nag Hammadi Library: A collection of Gnostic texts discovered in Egypt in 1945, providing invaluable insights into early Christian and Gnostic thought.

Patristic: Relating to the writings of the early Church Fathers.

Qumran: An archaeological site near the Dead Sea, famous for the discovery of the Dead Sea Scrolls, which shed light on Jewish and early Christian sects.

References

The following works were consulted and cited in the preparation of this book. A comprehensive list is provided to allow readers to further explore the historical and theological context of the Gospel of the Hebrews.

Bauer, W. (1996). Orthodoxy and heresy in earliest Christianity (R. A. Kraft & G. Krodel, Eds.; 2nd ed.). Sigler Press.

Crossan, J. D. (1993). The historical Jesus: The life of a Mediterranean Jewish peasant. HarperCollins.

Ehrman, B. D., & Plese, Z. (2014). *The other gospels: Accounts of Jesus from outside the New Testament*. Oxford University Press.

Pagels, E. H. (1991). *The gnostic gospels*. Vintage Books.

Perkins, P. (1994). *Gnosticism and the new testament*. Fortress Press.

Robertson, J. M. (1990). *The Nag Hammadi Library in English*. Harper & Row, Publishers.

Schneemelcher, W. (Ed.). (1991). *New testament apocrypha* (R. M. Wilson, Trans.). J. Clarke & Co., Westminster/John Knox Press.